Siked

Siked

Samuel David Drew

PALMETTO

P U B L I S H I N G

Charleston, SC

www.PalmettoPublishing.com

Samuel Drew email: sdd501@jagmail.southalabama.edu

Hardcover ISBN: 9798822956797
Paperback ISBN: 9798822956803
eBook ISBN: 9798822956810

To all of the homeless mentally ill who were deinstitutionalized through a series of events beyond their control.

Table of Contents

CHAPTER 1

A Harsh Beginning

Johnny B. was born in New York City and considered a savant by most experts in the field of psychology. The psychiatrist that he had seen in the past had rated his IQ above the genius level, but he had also diagnosed Johnny with schizophrenia in his young adulthood. Johnny was born at St. E's Hospital where his mother left him a couple of days after giving birth. She placed him on the steps of the hospital and ran away, hoping that someone would find him. She hid herself in the foliage surrounding the facility and watched. One of the nurses that was getting off duty noticed the infant crying on the steps and came to the rescue. It did not take long, and Johnny was safe back in the facility in familiar surroundings. This eased his anxiety at the time, but he did not know how far he had to go. As the old nursery rhyme goes:

> Monday's child is fair of face, Tuesday's child is
> full of grace,
> Wednesday's child is full of woe, Thursday's child
> has far to go,
> Friday's child is loving and giving, Saturday's child
> works hard for his living,

And the child that is born on the Sabbath day
Is bonny and blithe, and good and gay.

(Sited from the internet website Monday's Child –
Nursery Rhymes (allnurseryrhymes.com),
01/23/2022 @ 12:42 p.m.)

Johnny was born on a Thursday, and the old nursery rhyme fit his life to a fault. The state was granted the responsibility of caring for him and placed him in a Catholic institution for orphans in the inner city. The facility had a good reputation at the time for providing a good education and meeting the orphans' daily necessities. The nuns took good care of Johnny and carefully watched his academic achievements within their institution. He was indoctrinated into the catholic religion, and as he grew up, he made friends with the instructors who were associated with the catholic organization. Some of the nuns noted that he was a little different than the other children, but that made them love him even more. They had high expectations for their little man and doted on him more than all the other orphans at the facility.

Although he was a well-mannered boy, he was out of touch with reality and had imaginary friends that did not dissipate as he grew into adulthood. The hallucinations appeared to be getting worse as he was preparing to go to college. It was a hard decision, but when Johnny reached his late teens, the priest over the school thought it was in everyone's best interest for Johnny to be admitted into an asylum that was affiliated with the catholic church for his own best interest. The priest feared that eventually Johnny might become a person who would harm himself or others.

At the asylum, Johnny learned how to manipulate the system of psychiatric care using the staff's testing, psychotherapy, and medication against them without anyone being the wiser. He was a good observer of the psychiatrists and their many different methods of attempting to heal the mentally ill. He was particularly caught up with the idea of hypnosis. He imagined that this form of therapy could help patients who suffered from the most untreatable forms of mental illness that were otherwise left unattended and locked away, due to the profession's inability to care for these patients. In the asylum, Johnny was given shelter, taught a trade, and had his necessities met.

CHAPTER 2

Moving Forward in the World of Rejects

As Johnny grew up into an adult, he was taught how to work on the theater set at the institution which included making costumes, providing makeup, instruction on memorization, and setting up props. He especially excelled in the areas of makeup, stage décor, and accents from different countries, to help the producers establish a more real experience for their audience. The asylum gave performances to help offset the expenses not acquired from the Federal or State Government and to keep the patients occupied during their stay.

The community totally supported the asylum with contributions to the theater, automobile repair, catering, and carpentry. Some of the people in the area were helped financially because the price for labor beat any competition, and they felt good about doing a service for the mental health profession in this small way. Although the community tried to support the asylum, the patient population grew due to the ending of WW2, the Korean War, and the Vietnam War. Also, there was a significant increase in the population of the U.S. which we call the baby boomers generation. The asylums tried to stay open by hiring staff that were more reasonable but less qualified. Also, they cut back on nutritional standards, trade classes, and allowed some of the patients to oversee other patients. It all added up to a disastrous outcome that took its toll on the institutions across America.

CHAPTER 3

The Community Mental Healthcare Act

In 1964 deinstitutionalization took a toll on the asylums across America, and Johnny was placed once again in the care of the Catholic organization. The Catholic Society for Adults (CSA) was a type of community mental healthcare center that the federal government recognized and supported with funds to provide for those individuals with mental issues who had spent the majority of their adult life in an institution. The idea of community-based assistance for the mentally ill was a sound idea, and it worked in parts of Europe that are more isolated and less prejudiced about the mentally ill. In the U.S., it was still in its infant stage, and the growing pains overcame the need of the individual. The American public was not quite ready to have psychologically disturbed individuals living next door or down the street from them.

Due to political agendas, community outcry, a lack of funding, an increase in the cost of food, shelter, medication, and professional healthcare providers, the community healthcare facilities were forced to push their patients out of the facility earlier than projected. This caused an influx of homeless individuals to hit the street in search of a home that could help them meet their necessities. These people who faced this dilemma needed help but had nowhere to turn except the homeless population in our cities. This practice continues even today, as we all have become so apathetic to this group of Americans; we should realize that if not for the grace of God, there go we. Without any family to turn to, Johnny soon found himself homeless and had nowhere to go.

CHAPTER 4

The Label of the Homeless

After surviving a horrific year on the streets of New York, Johnny began to repeat his activity. After all, we are all creatures of habit. His reality became a vicious cycle of either being arrested for vagrancy, placed in prison for thirty days, put in the infirmary for his condition, given meds, and provided therapy until he was discharged back onto the street. He thought that this was a similar experience that he had had when he was in the asylum. On some occasions he would be picked up by an ambulance service who had been called by a concerned citizen. Johnny would catch the flu or the common cold which could turn into pneumonia when not treated timely.

Once in the hospital, it did not take long before the staff realized that Johnny was mentally ill. He would be placed on the mentally ill ward, provided meds, receive therapy, and discharged back onto the street. His imaginary friends helped him get through these difficult situations, and he leaned on them for support through it all. Pneumonia, bronchitis, or the flu usually found its way into the homeless population, and without immediate care from the local hospital, these individuals would not live through the course of the disease process. Johnny went to the hospital or the city jail where he was processed, fed, given shelter, and provided medication to help him with his psychosis. He often thought of these institutions as a different form of an asylum.

When he met the release criteria, he was discharged and placed back on the street until the next visit was recorded. This routine is known in psychology circles as the revolving door syndrome and continues with the homeless today. This syndrome is a drain on resources in many cities across the United States. The State eventually came up with a plan to decrease the homeless population in their state. Due to the high cost of unpaid hospital bills, law enforcement, and being a blot on society's landscape, Johnny and several other homeless individuals were loaded up on a bus with one-way tickets to Pennsylvania, Maryland, or any place outside the current state's jurisdiction. A few months later, he was placed on another bus and relocated to Virginia.

Over the next few months, Johnny found himself being bused from place to place until he reached his unforeseen destination in Mobile, Alabama. It was raining hard with intermittent lightning and thunder when he arrived. He quickly took refuge under an interstate bridge with a lot of other homeless individuals, which included women and children. All these individuals had hopes and dreams of making it in society someday. They were human beings living in inhumane conditions. Johnny did not mind the overcrowding conditions he found himself in under the bridge, but he did regret seeing small children sick, malnourished, shoeless, and sleeping with a parent in fear of what tomorrow might bring. He dreamed of a day when he would be able to help all homeless individuals, but for now he could not even help himself.

CHAPTER 5

Living on the Gulf Coast

Johnny liked living in Mobile, Alabama, on the bay with its sunshine, warm climate, history, hospitality, and most of all its fishing accessibility. It appeared to be a homeless person's paradise through the eyes of America's most devastated people. He was able to get scraps from the local restaurants and donations from people who passed him by at Bienville Square to help with his daily needs. Johnny's days were long and consistent with a trip downtown or a short walk to the causeway. He could spend a summer day lying about on the seawall by the interstate and work on his tan. Relaxing in the sun and forgetting about his problems became commonplace during the long hot summer days.

He had many adventures with his imaginary friends that continued to be an important part of his life. They would walk and talk with Johnny to his different destinations throughout the downtown area of Mobile. He would sometimes listen to the waves lapping up against the seawall, which were very comforting and could lull Johnny to sleep for a short nap in the middle of the day. At night he slept with many other homeless people under the I-10 bridge in downtown Mobile. Someone would start a fire right before dark in several fifty-gallon drums, and everyone would pitch in food that they had acquired throughout the day or purchased with donations provided by the general population. It was never a banquet, but it was enough to sustain life for all the group, young and old. Everyone appreciated a good meal at the end of a difficult day on the gulf coast.

Some of the homeless had musical instruments and others could sing. After having their supper, many of the people under the bridge would sing songs popular at the time. Blues, rock and roll, country, and gospel songs could be heard for miles around. It gave a very good impression of a bright future with prosperity just around the corner. Jubilees would happen on occasion, and the homeless population would have a seafood smorgasbord for a night or two which always provided strength and hope within the community. A jubilee was noted as a change in the water oxygen content which caused all marine life to run aground onto the shore.

The usual locations to find this anomaly were on Dauphin Island or Fairhope which had a perfect shore for the event to take place. Residents could then walk around with a pall of some sort and collect all the fish, crabs, and shrimp that they could carry. There was never any kind of warning when the event would take place, but it would happen, and it was a lucky break for those who were in the right place at the right time.

Occasionally Johnny would have a deep discussion with his hallucinations. Many people would find him odd and a little frightening at times. Eventually everyone seemed to accept Johnny and his strange ways under the I-10 bridge. At the end of the day, the sunset always resulted in a feeling of peace and contentment within the homeless population. Although they were homeless and had no way of knowing what tomorrow would be like, they still thanked God for his blessings upon them.

Over the short time that Johnny had been at this location, he had acquired three good friends who often ventured out into the city to see what type of accommodations were offered in Mobile for the homeless. These three comrades would leave, and be gone for a few days, but they always made it back under the bridge to share their stories of adventure. It was the big news of the day, and it often offered many people hope of the possibility of a better future. Their names were Sam, David, and Ronnie, and on one occasion they had been out exploring in West Mobile when they stumbled onto a university with a free psychiatric clinic. They were able to write down the location of the clinic for future reference just in case they needed to come back to the clinic.

When they came back to camp, they told Johnny about the free psychiatric clinic at a university no more than five miles from where they were. He was the first person they thought of when they found the clinic because they knew of his mental illness. He had confided in their discretion as friends and explained to them his set of circumstances. They were very excited to tell Johnny that the clinic was located at the corner of Old Jack Street and Union Bay Road. It might take a couple of hours to walk that distance, but it could be worth the effort for him. Johnny thanked his three friends and took the copy of the directions that they had given him and put it in his pocket with the idea of leaving for the clinic as soon as possible.

CHAPTER 6

A New Day

Johnny became so excited with the idea that he wanted to leave right away. He was once again starting to have visions of grandeur, and his hallucinations were becoming so real, he was having a hard time separating his mental psychosis from reality. He knew he needed to get help from a psychiatrist as soon as possible if he wanted to stay out of jail or the hospital. He felt like this could be his chance to receive prescribed medications that could help him with his mental disorder and his hallucinations. He was constantly plagued with hallucinations of a mother who was never there, a best friend named Jimmy who was always getting Johnny into trouble, and an imaginary father he never knew.

When he was young, he would make up stories and have many fantasies about someone showing up at the orphanage from a wealthy estate to take him home to a mansion. As he grew up, this developed into imaginative friends and family who became more real at times than the people he knew in the real world. These were individuals that he saw consistently, and the only thing that stopped the verbal or visual hallucinations was pharmaceuticals. The very next day Johnny took his friends' directions that they had written down on a brown paper bag and started out on what was to be his greatest adventure.

After a couple of hours of hiking around the city with the provided directions, he was standing in front of the free clinic for the mentally ill. He walked into the clinic when a loud alarm went off, signaling a new patient had entered the building. Embarrassed, he quickly signed the roster and had a seat in the lobby with the other patients. Everyone in the clinic had become used to the alarm, and they showed no attention to the newcomer. He sat nervously in the corner and watched everyone else as they moved in and out of the room. Eventually, the nurse came to the door and called his name.

He walked through the swinging doors and down a long hall to an office, situated in the back of the building. His vital signs were taken, his weight, and a quick questionnaire was filled out to make sure he qualified for assistance from the clinic. Dr. S. entered the room with a folder in his hand that had Johnny's name on it. He sat down alongside Johnny and the conversation began. Johnny had heard these same words many times before and knew how to answer every question to get what he wanted. He also had seen all the pictured inkblots many times before and knew what to say to be compliant. Johnny wanted to make a good first impression with the doctor to receive the help he needed. The medication to help him with his hallucinations was his focus throughout the process.

He could use a place of his own to take him out of the elements, and a job to help him meet his needs. It would be awesome to have a place of his own and not have to dig in garbage cans to have food to eat, but in his mind's eye he could not get away from the visions of little children living homeless in the streets of the Port City he now called home. He continued to manipulate the conversation, and Dr. S. did exactly what Johnny wanted him to do. Dr. S, went to a locked cabinet in the room and gave Johnny some samples of medications, provided to the clinic by the pharmaceutical sales rep, for his schizophrenia until he could get his prescriptions filled. He also referred him to a social worker for further evaluation and assistance. Johnny was provided a bottle of water, and he used it to wash down his medication without any complications.

He had been given these medications before and had no issue with using them again. Soon the hallucinations dissipated, and he found a moment of clarity, which always seemed to cause a change in his life. Sometimes the change was good and sometimes not so much, but a change usually always followed the beginning of using the medications provided to him.

CHAPTER 7

Time for a Change

The social worker assigned to Johnny's case was Mrs. C., and Dr. S. felt like Johnny needed to see her immediately to get the assistance he needed for a better quality of life with a better outcome. He took the necessary steps to make sure the appointment was scheduled, and Johnny was soon on his way to becoming a more complete person with dreams, desires, compassion, love, and happiness that we all take for granted throughout our lifespan. Johnny was not an alien from another planet; he was a human being with mental illness, and he was smart.

Johnny's appointment with Mrs. C. was immediate or so it seemed, and he was on time, waiting in her office. She was located on Spring Set Boulevard which was closer to the I-10 bridge. He noticed how beautiful was Mrs. C's smile, blonde hair, blue eyes, medium built, and deep, strong voice that was equivalent to some men he had known. All her features took him by surprise, and Johnny thought to himself that she could have sung baritone at the local church if she desired. He found her very attractive and imagined himself hanging out with her if the situation was different. She and Johnny became good friends and worked together to find him a job at the university in the maintenance department on the evening shift after everyone had gone home. She also found him a small, one-bedroom apartment within walking distance of his job which proved to be very convenient.

So, Johnny worked in the maintenance department and became a good custodial worker at the university, performing simple tasks daily. His main job was to clean the classrooms, bathrooms, offices, and study halls within the campus to the best of his ability. He also was required to check in with Mrs. C. once a week to go over possible goals, to reevaluate his progress, and to discuss any issues that needed to be addressed. Also, Dr. S. had to keep a record of his progress that Mrs. C. sent to him every month. He was scheduled to see Dr. S. in six months. His shift started promptly at 3 p.m. and ended at 11 p.m., with a time clock keeping an account of all the hours he had worked. He had no supervisor on his job, and he liked the autonomy that it provided. Johnny wanted to succeed at his new occupation, and he came in early every scheduled shift.

On the evening shift, he had complete access to all the universities with a master key that opened all doors with one exception. He could not get into the president's office, and he recognized this was off limits to him. Although it made him curious, he did not want to jeopardize his job over such a trivial thing as that. He was now his own boss, and when everyone else had gone home, he was still there to walk freely throughout the university into different areas of the college at his leisure. He enjoyed the arts and the drama department best because of its unusual atmosphere and different genres of art displayed on the walls. The drama department had quite a collection of paintings and photos of artists from past performances. Sometimes Johnny could take his break in the drama department when there was a play performing, and he could enjoy a little of the performance as he ate his sandwich.

Life was good and he had to pinch himself from time to time just to make sure he was not dreaming. Some of his favorite plays included *A Midsummer Night's Dream* and *A Funny Thing Happened on The Way to The Forum*. After the plays were concluded, Johnny would admire some of the very talented local artists who had performed at the university's auditorium. Sometimes, Sam, David, and Ronnie would stop by to see how Johnny was getting along. They also used this time to discuss some new information they had acquired in their travels. After their visit, Johnny would give them a little money to use to help the children under the bridge. He still had memories of seeing those half-naked, hungry children sleeping with their parents in fear of the next day.

Their visit allowed Johnny the chance to entertain guests at his apartment, which was a big part of his psychological therapy. He kept a journal and documented his guests' arrival and departure times, which he would turn into the case worker to show his compliance with his new life. For the first time in his life, Johnny was beginning to feel the need to comply with rules and the possibility of succeeding in a vocation which he took great pride in. He recalled the advice the priest overseeing the orphanage gave him before he left for the asylum. "Remember, Johnny, to be the best in your vocation no matter what it is. I don't care if you become a ditch digger; just be the best ditch digger you can be."

He took pride in his occupation, accomplishments, and the life he was leading. There was only one problem: he continued to have visions of grandeur, and he wanted more out of life than the mediocre life that had been dealt him. Although he was just a janitor, he took pride in his work and received a paycheck every week that allowed him to pay his bills, buy staples, and supply some of his homeless friends with food and clothing. His focus was on the children and how to supply their needs that would give them hope for tomorrow and keep them healthy. This ideology exacerbated his psychosis and made him feel like he could achieve anything or be anyone he wanted to be.

CHAPTER 8

Curiosity or Fate

Late at night, when Johnny was all alone in the psychology department, he would look through the patient's files out of curiosity and to try and better understand himself with case studies similar to his own. He remembered all the information verbatim because he had a photographic memory. It was a serious invasion of privacy, but who would ever suspect him if he kept the information confidential? After all, he was just one of the janitors with no reason to be curious. One night while Johnny was working in the psychology department, he began his regular routine of looking through the files of the patients when he found some new mail with an unopened letter addressed to Dr. S. He glanced over the envelope and noticed the letter had originated from Switzerland. Johnny was tempted to look at it since it was from another country, and curiosity can overtake any feeling of privacy in a situation like this. Who could this be? What does this letter hold in it from Switzerland? Johnny's curiosity overtook him, and he had to look inside. God works in mysterious ways.

CHAPTER 9

An Idea is Born

The letter was from a famous psychiatrist named Dr. D. Johnny had figured out a way to use steam to open letters when he was in the asylum, and his curiosity got the best of him. He stuffed the letter into his back pocket for safekeeping until he could get home. After all, the doctor who the letter was addressed to called out sick for the day and never knew of the letter being delivered. So, Johnny hurried home after his shift and used a pot of boiling water to produce the steam that allowed him to open the letter and see the contents inside without ripping the envelope, just in case he needed to return the letter to its proper destination. Afterward he could reseal the letter with some glue, and no one would ever know he had peaked at the letter. This letter from Dr. D. stated:

Dear Dr. S. and faculty at the University Psychology Clinic.

Greetings from Switzerland. I hope that this letter finds you and your staff well. About the offer you have extended to me, I regretfully must decline the post of Professor of Psychiatric Medicine/Clinical

Physician at this time. Due to my present situation here at home, I am forced to let this great opportunity pass by. I hope we can continue to consult each other on future cases and research that could lead to breakthroughs in modern psychiatric medicine.

Sincerely your colleague in psychiatric medicine,
Dr. D., MD of Psychiatry

This letter struck a chord in Johnny's mind and a plan began to develop. It was similar to a student taking his first philosophy class, when his head begins to tickle due to all the deep information he/she learns on their journey into enlightenment, just beyond nirvana. He liked the idea and the prospect of pretending to be a psychiatrist. He could do this without question. He had been to so many psychiatrists that he knew how to psychoanalyze and prescribe medication for many different psychoses. He thought that if he had a license, he could help people just as well as any psychiatrist. He took the letter and scanned it to make the necessary adjustments until he got what he wanted. He had learned in one of the community mental healthcare facilities that he could scan a document, use a keyboard to delete, and rewrite whatever he wanted. He used this technique to rewrite Dr. D.'s letter and the following was the result:

Greetings Dr. S. and all the faculty at the University.

I humbly accept your offer as the Professor of Psychiatric Medicine/Clinical Physician at your school and look forward to meeting you in person after my long journey to the United States of America. It will take me a couple of months to prepare for the voyage from Zurich, Switzerland, and to get my paperwork together so I can get through customs in a timely manner. I will see you as soon as I am able to resolve any issues that might hamper my process and goal of working side by side with you.

Sincerely,
Dr. D., Doctor of Psychiatry.

Johnny signed the letter as Dr. D., resealed it, and placed it in Dr. S.'s incoming mailbox. Johnny was excited about the possibility of practicing as a doctor of psychiatry; he could not sleep that night. He knew that he did not look like someone from Switzerland, so he would need a disguise. The college of art and drama would give him the perfect opportunity to achieve the objective he was looking for. He could acquire small pieces of makeup, wardrobe, wigs, beards, and a cassette tape which taught actors how to speak with a Switzerland accent. If he took the items in small quantities over time no one would even notice.

Johnny knew he had to prepare for his new role and occupation within a short time frame. He faced some hard questions that would have to be answered if he wanted to succeed in his task. What were his goals? What were his obstacles? The way he saw it his goals were simple:

1. Acquire the necessary things he needed for his new identity.

2. Practice to perfection the accent from the tape to help with his disguise.
3. Find a new apartment where he could entertain guests and show his influence on the world in a type of psychosocial aspect that would be expected with his new identity.
4. Work on his gait and mannerisms as to not give even a little hint of who he really was.
5. Think ahead of questions that might destroy his train of thought and/or give way to an all-out confession that would be unforgivable by a man like Dr. S. and the university. This was serious and could lead to jail time.

His obstacles did not present themselves as quickly, and it required a little more thought into the process:

1. He would have to abandon his job as a janitor.
2. He would have to portray his new identity all the time.
3. He would have to disappear from the weekly visits that Mrs. C. made in a way that would not cause any suspicion.
4. He would have to go over the files of the patients a little closer to continue the documented therapy and treatment that had sustained those clients over the previous years.

CHAPTER 10

The Transformation

Johnny began to prepare himself for the role of Dr. D. with all urgency. He practiced every moment of his spare time on his accent, and he checked out books on Switzerland, their language, history, and their people. He also studied their approach to psychiatry, which included different approaches to the mentally ill, practice, research, and accomplishments. After a couple of months, it was time to move forward, and he was confident that he was ready to enter the realm of psychiatry with his new persona. After all, he had been a patient of psychiatry all his life, and it was intriguing to think that now he had the chance to be on the other side of the practice.

Johnny B. transformed himself into Dr. D. with a wig of blonde hair, a matching goatee glued to his face, a white shirt, a red tie, and a navy blue suit that he had acquired from the university's lost and found. With one last longing look, Johnny became Dr. D. within a blink of an eye, and he was amazed at the transformation. When he looked at himself in the mirror, he did not recognize his reflection, and with one more quick look at his disguise, he left for the clinic. It was not a look of narcissism but more of a final look over before going into his next great adventure.

Upon his arrival at the clinic, he was immediately greeted by the receptionist who was working her way through college to become a nurse. "Hi, my name is Ms. W., and you must be Dr. D." Johnny felt a spark of fear come over him and he started to get anxious. He could have just darted back out of the door and ran away, but thanks to the medications for concentration that Dr. S. had prescribed him, he was able to calm himself and keep his composure.

He replied, "Yes, I am Dr. D., and I am here to work at the university," in a strong Swedish accent that surprised even himself.

Ms. W. smiled and said, "Dr. S. is waiting for you in his office; he has been expecting you, Dr. D." That was the first time he had been shown any respect and admiration; it caused his heart to beat irregularly for a moment. He knew he was having a panic attack, but he settled down, greeted Dr. S. with a smile, and in the usual manner of politeness seen within the scope of normal conversation.

"Hello, I am Dr. S., and I welcome you to the university and the United States of America." He noticed how young and familiar Dr. D. looked and caught himself staring at his new partner.

Dr. D. stared back and said, "Can I help you? Because you seem to be staring hard at me for some reason. Dr. S. regained his composure and said he felt like they had met somewhere before. Dr. S. thought to himself that something was all too familiar about him and his mannerisms. Dr. S. mentioned that maybe they had met previously at a seminar or on some coincidental holiday. Dr. D. smiled and said, "Maybe we have; one never knows, and the world is getting smaller every day."

Dr. S. invited him into his office where they could work out some of the awkward details of his new position. He signed a contract that stated he would receive two hundred thousand dollars a year and a ten percent bonus at the end of each quarter if he met the patient quota. Also, if he found any new therapeutic techniques, invented a new device, or discovered a new procedure, all the benefits would fall back to the university. His benefits were the usual major medical, dental, eye care, and retirement in a stock held by the American Psychological Association (APA) that was entirely paid for by the university. He also had a golden umbrella clause that paid him his salary and benefits for three years after separating from the institution.

In return for such a grand package, the university would need him to work in the lecture hall on Monday, Wednesday, and Friday where he would teach medical students from 7 a.m. to 9 p.m. with an hour lunch break from 12–1pm. Tuesday and Thursday he could help Dr. S. with clinical treatment for the mentally ill population in the local area. Dr. S. asked Dr. D. if he knew that in the U.S. over fifty percent of all homeless individuals have some form of mental illness. Dr. S. continued, "I think that it is unacceptable for a country that has forty percent of the world's wealth, but only six percent of the world's population, to allow its citizens to be treated with such demise and abandonment. What is your opinion on the subject, Dr. D.?"

He just shook his head in agreement and said, with a strong Swedish accent, "We are going to get along splendidly because I feel the same way. I have studied the U.S.'s problems concerning their mentally ill population, which includes those found to be homeless. This subject material is at the top of my list for research and development." Dr. D. continued, "Asylums provide a basic need in our society, even though they have been closed across the country. The proof is in the pudding, and people with mental illnesses have been victimized by society. Working together, maybe we can provide evidence and write a proposal to the U.S. Government in hope of reopening or rebuilding some of the asylums that have been abandoned."

Dr. S. disagreed with Dr. D.'s ideology. Dr. S. said that asylums were too expensive, torturous, in need of repairs, and usually ended up not helping mentally ill patients. He also said that in some cases people were tortured, killed, or lobotomized for no apparent reason. Dr. S. explained that through a discussion about their problems, showing genuine compassion, and acknowledging respect to each individual, the field might make a bigger impact on the patients. "Medication should be used sparingly and only as a last resort. So many times, our colleagues want to prescribe medication and put them in a padded cell. This approach can become a crutch for the individual with no way out.

"The drugs can help make them more compliant with their therapy or surroundings, which enables them to find their groove in society. But we must remember the words of the billionaire Paul Getty who said, 'Beware of thinking you have found your groove, for a groove will soon wear into a rut, and a rut will wear into a grave.' With psychiatric pharmaceutical therapy, patients can find their groove which can follow Getty's theoretical pattern. We must be careful how we approach our research and conclusions with this subject matter due to the society that we live in. I will help you all I can concerning the homeless mentally ill after our clinical hours, but I just want to let you know up front that I am against reopening the asylums."

After the discussion, Dr. S. asked for Dr. D's credentials, stating that he never received his license of psychiatry from Switzerland,

and it would need to be presented as soon as possible. Dr. D. had prepared for such a question and responded without hesitation. Dr. D. said in Switzerland things are processed a little slower and as soon as he had it in hand, he would bring it in. But if it was totally necessary, he would just stay in a nearby hotel, and when it came in, he would bring it in. Dr. S. wanted to wait for the credentials, but against his better judgment, and realizing how busy the clinic was and the increased student population for that semester, he told Dr. D. to begin orientation the next day.

The two shook hands, and Dr. D. went straight home to get ready for his evening shift as a janitor at the university. He had to keep up the charade as long as possible or he would be exposed rather quickly. The consequences of that would have been too terrible to imagine, so he geared himself up for another evening shift at the university. His shift went by very quickly, and he went straight home and slept well with the alarm clock set for 6:00 a.m. The clock went off and Johnny sprang out of bed like a little boy excited about his first day at school. He put his disguise on, grabbed his briefcase, and headed to the clinic.

CHAPTER 11

First Day at the Clinic

Dr. S. had not arrived at the clinic yet, so the nurse introduced herself to Dr. D. She began her introduction by saying, "Hello, my name is Ms. B." Dr. D. could not help but notice how beautiful Ms. B. was. Her hair was long, autumn red, she had blue eyes, a dark tan, and her body had an hourglass shape to it that was striking.

Johnny kept his composure and responded by saying, in his Swedish accent, "Hello, my name is Dr. D. I have just arrived from Switzerland and look forward to working closely with you to help our patients."

Ms. B. smiled warmly and said, "Yes, I know who you are, and if you follow me, I will show you to your office and around the clinic." The orientation was quick, to the point, and Dr. D. knew where everything was within a few minutes. She gave him his lab coat, which already had his name and credentials on it, and a stamp for prescriptions that was used by his predecessor. Dr. D. was taking the place of Dr. J., and Ms. B. thought that it would be convenient to use the previous doctor's medical stamp for prescriptions until Dr. D.'s paperwork could be acquired and processed from Switzerland.

Dr. J. had recently suffered a heart attack and was out on a permanent leave of absence. The university was calling his absence a sabbatical, but he was facing an early retirement due to health reasons which put the clinic in a bind. Some of the patients had not been seen for at least six months, and new clients were being sent over daily from the local hospitals and clinics. When Ms. B. was confident that Dr. D. knew the basic scope of the office, location of the supplies, and the paperwork associated with the office, so she opened the doors. The patients began to march in, and the staff took their places in the clinic.

CHAPTER 12

The Case of Big Dan

Dr. D's first patient was named Dan, and he suffered from a type of antisocial personality disorder with a tendency for depression. Dan introduced himself nervously to Dr. D. and sat in the leather chair in front of the desk. As the session began, Dr. D. remembered how he felt when he had been on the receiving end of many psychoanalyzing sessions; he knew how the inquiry should go.

First, he had Dan lay down on the leather couch, and Dr. D. took his place in the chair behind the couch where Dan could not see him. Dr. D. would ask Dan to clear his mind of any stressful thoughts and just say anything that comes to mind. "Don't overthink any of the questions; just go with it and tell me what is on your mind." Dr. D. felt so much excitement throughout his person he could hardly contain himself. He was in total control of the situation through his own volition, and he enjoyed every moment of the session. "Why do you feel depressed?" asked Dr. D.

Dan replied that he had some issues in his life that were beyond his control, and he did not know how to cope with it. Dan continued to discuss how he didn't like being around most people but felt a need to be accepted in society. He also stated that this made him sad, and this sadness developed into a depressive state. Dr. D.

encouraged Dan, "Continue to explain, and try to provide me some more details on how it makes you feel."

"My wife after thirty years of marriage has left me for a younger man, my job is a dead end, and I am turning sixty with no retirement to sustain me until I reach the end of my life. I am overweight and feel that my demise is close at hand. Can you help me?"

Dr. D. just stared at the picture on the wall and said, "I see. So, what you're trying to say is that you are depressed because your life is depressing, and you see no future."

"Yes," said Dan, "You are exactly right."

"Please continue, Dan. I might be able to help you."

Dan continued, "I have had some thoughts of suicide and cannot seem to shake the idea."

"So, you feel tormented, and if you would end your life everything would be better." Dan answered his question quickly and to the point with a yes. Dr. D. said, "Please continue."

"Well, I had been ill with pneumonia and was admitted to the university's hospital for pulmonary care when the nurse caught me in the bathroom trying to hang myself with a sheet."

Dr. D held back his emotions and said, "I see. Please continue."

"The pulmonologist noted that I was suffering from a case of extreme depression and prescribed me some antidepressants with a consult to this clinic. That is why I am here today."

Dr. D. replied, "I see. So what you are saying is that because you failed in your attempt to kill yourself, you have been sent here to undergo a complete psychiatric workup in an attempt to go through the rest of your life as normal as possible."

"Yes, that is correct, as normal as possible."

"Well, Dan, I really do think I can help you. I am going to prescribe you some new antidepressants that work better with less side effects and a 1000-piece puzzle of the ocean waves that I found in the clinic. I am also sending you over to physical therapy to help you with starting up an exercise routine. Remember not to disregard exercise because it is very helpful to the overall health of the human being. Here is a sample of the antidepressants that I have prescribed for you, but you will need to fill your prescription as soon as you can. Dan, I want to see you in three months with this puzzle completed and glued to the back of a plywood frame. You will hang it on a wall that will be visible every day as you wake up from your slumber. It will be a testament to your achievement and steadfastness.

"Also, I want you to record your weight over the next three months, and we will talk about it when I see you at your next appointment." Dr. D. made it perfectly clear that if this does not improve his state of mind that electroconvulsive shock therapy (ECT) might be the next step. Dr. D. asked Dan if he knew what ECT was and if he would like him to explain the procedure. Dan replied that he had heard of it, but he would rather not know what it was unless it became necessary. Dr. D. encouraged Dan to take up walking, running, biking, or some other type of exercise along with his physical therapy. "Your body is strong enough to perform this type of strenuous activity. You are just a little deconditioned, so let's get you back on track with some cardiovascular exercise. This could accelerate you getting back to a healthy state of mind."

Dr. D. and Dan talked for about an hour on subjects of less importance; for example, who is going to win the World Series, how to drive a sixteen-penny nail with a hammer, and the high cost of living in such a rich country. After the session, Dr. D. walked Dan to the door, gave him the prescription, and said, "I will see you in three months." Dan left the clinic with a big smile on his face and quickness in his step. He felt better than he had in a long time, and it was all due to his new psychiatrist Dr. D.

Dr. D. saw a few more patients, and then it was time for lunch. Dr. S. came by Dr. D.'s office to see if he would like to join him for lunch, but Dr. D. declined the invitation and took the opportunity to study his office space with a little more curiosity as he ate his peanut butter and jelly sandwich. Johnny's experience as a patient had provided him with insight not known, except within the walls of the asylums. He knew from his experience that psychiatrists usually left a few things behind to fulfill a type of professional courtesy to their replacement. Dr. J. had left Johnny a nice gift that would help him on his quest of helping others reach a more normal state of mind within their lifetime.

This was all subjective, Johnny thought, because what society sees as normal might be irregular to others, but the greater good must always be taken into consideration when seeking out the answer to this type of question. What is a normal state of mind and why is there so much at stake when we discuss such matters? Johnny was browsing throughout his office pondering over these thoughts and wondering, what did Dr. J. leave in the office to assist him with his current work? After a thorough investigation around the office, he gave up just in time for his next patient.

CHAPTER 13

The Amazing Ms. P.
and Her Vacation

Ms. P was announced by the nurse, and she entered the room in a beige dress that had been tailored to fit her current physique. According to her records, she had lost ten pounds in three months. At sixty-seven years of age, Ms. P. was in retirement and having a tough time coping with the change. She had been a professor at the university, and now she was a patient at the clinic for manic depression. She began the session with a little background about herself as expected from an ex-professor.

Dr. D. just sat behind her in the chair looking up at the ceiling fan and nodding in agreement with whatever she said. Suddenly, he noticed a gold coin on a chain hanging from the corner of a square frame on the wall by his desk. Of course, he thought to himself, this is the tool that Dr. J. had left behind to help him with his patients at the clinic. How had he missed such a beautiful medallion on a gold chain. It had to have been hiding behind that picture the whole time he was searching throughout the room for it. He picked it up gently and knew right away that his predecessor had left this piece of jewelry behind for him to use. This was the tool that was going to help him turn the field of psychiatry upside down.

He began to envision winning all kinds of awards but quickly came back to himself, seeing Ms. P. looking at him with a glare that took him back. Dr. D. broke the silence and told Ms. P. that he could help her, but he would need her undivided attention and cooperation in order to accelerate the healing process. She agreed to do whatever it took; she just wanted to feel better. Dr. D. picked up the piece of jewelry like a kid who picks up a new toy and waved it back and forth in front of his eyes. He then slowly moved it in front of her eyes and initiated the start of a hypnosis session. Dr. D. told Ms. P. to stare deep into the coin, now look one step beyond the coin.

"It will help you grow very sleepy, very sleepy, very sleepy. Just close your eyes, Ms. P. because your eyes are getting heavy, so heavy you must close them. Now clear your mind, relax, and drift off into a deep, deep sleep. You are going deeper, deeper, deeper into the darkness. You are trying to open your eyes, but you cannot because they are too heavy. You can only hear the sound of my voice, and you will concentrate on what I am saying. Nothing else matters at this point, just sleep and the sound of my voice, the sound of my voice.

"You are on a vacation, and it is a place that you have never been before. It has a beautiful setting with palm trees blowing in the wind, white sandy beaches, and the ocean water is so clear you can see your toes wiggling in the bottom of the water, stirring up the sand. You can see porpoises dancing in the water and seagulls are flying overhead. Can you see it Ms. P.?"

"Yes, yes, I can see everything you have described, and it is so beautiful."

"You can see your bungalow right on the beach. It has all the comforts of home and everything a person might need to have a most excellent vacation. Can you see it Ms. P.?"

"Yes, I see it all: a hammock, beach lounge chairs, tanning oil, and young men assisting me with all my needs. It is the perfect vacation that I have needed for such a long time. The sun is high in the sky and there is not a cloud anywhere. The waves lap onto the shore in a rhythm that can put me to sleep as I relax in my lounge chair."

"Ok, ok, now listen very closely. I want you to do whatever you enjoy the most on this vacation. Just let your mind go and do the thing that brings you total relaxation, comfort, and joy."

"Ok," she exclaimed excitedly. After about ten minutes into her session, Dr. D. would quietly enter the room to check on her progress and to make sure she was alright. He could hear her moaning with ecstasy or at times giggling like a little girl. She appeared to be enjoying herself throughout her vacation, and he became concerned he might not be able to bring her back. After all, this was the first time he had ever been in charge of any type of therapy, and he was a little more than anxious. At the end of the session, Dr. D. thought it would be best to bring her out of her hypnotic vacation state of mind. Dr. D. told her that when he snapped his fingers and clapped his hands that she would awaken with the memory of the most wonderful vacation. She had experienced a vacation that not only satisfied her mental state of being but also satisfied her physical being as well. Ms. P. left the clinic with a newness of mind and physical refreshment. She had been on a vacation in her mind and was ready to face the world again with new vigor. Dr. D. scheduled Ms. P. a follow up appointment in three months, and she seemed excited at the idea of coming back for her next session.

He saw approximately three more patients, and it was time to lock up the office and go home. He was so excited about his new-found identity and occupation that he did not want to quit seeing patients, but it was time to go home. Dr. D. said his farewells to his colleagues and headed back to his apartment in Haven Dale, enjoying every step of his walk along the sidewalk, remembering parts of a little rhyme, "don't step on a crack or you break your mama's back." He laughed to himself as he walked and thought how he had pulled it off. He had no formal education, but he was now a doctor of psychiatry. Wouldn't his mama be impressed with him if she only knew. His past was not going to hinder his future and his future was looking bright. Or was it? He started to feel a little paranoid and started to question himself and his situation. But it was a nice fall day, and all was well in his mind. He made the short walk to his home, took his medication, ate his supper, and went to bed.

CHAPTER 15

Class and Tammy B.

The next day he had the opportunity to teach a class in the medical school with a hands-on approach to psychotherapy. It was in this class that he met a young lady named Tammy B. who became the love of his life, although he did not know it at the time. She was a pretty woman, about twenty-one years old, and was working on her graduate classes while helping in the medical school program for psychiatry. She had long, strawberry blond hair that stopped at her waist, big pale blue eyes, porcelain skin, and a slender figure that exaggerated the fullness of her chest and butt. Dr. D. was taken back by her incredible features and started to question his emotional distress. What was wrong with him? Why did he feel this way about a woman he had never met before? The chemistry was there, pushing him to find out more about her.

She took one look at him and felt a strong desire to run up, hug him, kiss him, and be with him. She quickly suppressed her desires, but it took every bit of restraint on her part to calm herself. She, too, did not understand the pull, attraction, and strange effect he had on her. It was like two moths dancing around a lit candle which pulled them into the fire. The closer the moths got to the fire, the hotter they became, and so it was between Tammy and Dr.

D. Two people feeling the effects of love at first sight. The chemistry was very strong between them, and it was hard to contain their emotions. She had to ask herself what was going on and why was she drawn to this man? It was as though he held a magical spell on her. Her face felt flushed, extreme warmth flowed through her body, and she was weak in her knees.

Eventually, they were able to step up and introduce themselves. "Hi, my name is Tammy B., and I am your teacher assistant or TA for this class." Dr. D. looked at Tammy in a shy way and stuttered as he asked her what exactly is a TA exactly. He took her hand and kissed it, just as he had seen people do in the movies. The students could see the heartfelt greeting that their instructors were in the process of, and with awes and laughter, the class applauded their introduction. Tammy responded by pulling her hand away gently and stated, "Oh yeah, you are from Switzerland, and you are not familiar with our system or customs. The TA assists the professor with getting the class structured and researches activities that you deem appropriate at the time. I can grade papers, run errands, tutor, and monitor your class during testing sessions if you like. I look forward to working with you in class and during the research intervals," and she stuck out her hand to shake Dr. D's.

Dr. D. did not know what to say, so he just kind of stared at her and shook her hand. He thought that it was better that he did not speak, considering he did not have much to say, no experience with women, and he thought her to be a little too aggressive. "I guess we need to get busy teaching the class. Can you tell me where we are in our curriculum?"

Tammy responded with the courtesy shown to professors at the time, "Today is the first day of class for the spring semester. We are going over the syllabus and giving the first reading assignment."

Dr. D said, "Ok, that sounds like a good place to start." Tammy had prepared everything the night before and passed out the syllabus to all the students and sat down in a chair to the left of the stage designated for TA's. The auditorium was full of students with great expectations and eager to learn more about their chosen field of study. Dr. D. introduced himself and went over the paperwork word for word. The students had heard the TA say that Dr. D. was from Switzerland, and they were curious about that country. Due to time constraints, no one asked any questions and class was dismissed after the assignment was given. After the class, Tammy asked Dr. D. if he would like to get a coffee or something at the snack bar in the cafeteria.

"Yes, I would like that, Tammy, and maybe you could go over a little of what is expected of me during the class time." Dr. D.'s heart was racing as they strolled into the cafeteria, and Tammy could sense his discomfort. She tried to ease his nerves by smiling, talking about her day, her future, and asking him a lot of questions about Switzerland. Their hands touched accidentally as they walked, and a static electrical charge was sent through each of their bodies. They quickly pulled away and laughed about the incident, but deep down they were both curious about one another.

Tammy started the conversation asking Dr. D., how How is the weather in Switzerland?"

"Cold!" he exclaimed.

"How long have you practiced medicine?"

"Seven years. I was first a computer hacker for the government, but I went back to school and got into medicine. I studied psychology firsthand in an asylum and always wanted to move to the U.S. due to their strong research programs for the homeless. You have lots of specimens which I can study from all walks of life. When the opportunity came, I took it and hoped that I could use my experience to help others going through a difficult time in their life."

Out of the blue, not realizing what she was saying, Tammy asked, "Are you married?"

"No," Dr. D. responded. "I have not had time for a wife with school, and my practice. Life has been a somewhat lonely endeavor for me."

This made Tammy happy, but she wondered what he could be thinking after she asked him a question like that. She continued her interrogation and asked him why he looked so young. "Psychiatrists usually are older and not so pleasant to the eyes, or so it seems. So how have you been able to keep such a youthful appearance? I hope you do not mind me asking. I have never seen a psychiatrist so young and good looking. I apologize if you have caught me staring at you, but it just strikes me as strange."

"I get that a lot, but I am not as young or inexperienced as I look. I have just taken good care of myself over the years, and it has paid off. In Switzerland the air is very clean, unlike cities in the U.S. like New York or Los Angeles. The lifestyle is also very healthy with lots of opportunity for exercise and a lean diet of fish and vegetables. This benefits everyone, which helps them look younger than they really are." Tammy was astonished with his answer and found it curious that a man of his caliber could be so kind and down to earth. She wondered if this was love at first sight, but without really knowing it, she was in fact falling in love with him. They had their coffee at the donut shop on campus, discussed a plan for the class infrastructure, and left with thoughts and expectations that are seen only when young adults fall in love.

CHAPTER 16

Mrs. L.

Dr. D. came to work the next day at 0730 on the dot, had a cup of coffee, and received his first patient at 0800. "Mrs. L. is here to see you, doctor," the nurse exclaimed.

"Yes, please show her in." Mrs. L. was a paranoid person who lived with her mother in a very depressed area of town. When she grew up in that area and her father was still alive, that part of town was highly desirable, but over the years it had become overrun by crime and a depressed psychosocial economy. She took odd jobs here and there, but she never managed to make enough money to get her out of the poverty level. Because of her inability to make a good salary, due to a set of unfortunate events, she was forced to live with her mother. It was not an agreeable situation but a force of necessity. Today was her first day at the clinic, and she did not know what to expect.

Everyone in the clinic seemed to want her dead or they wanted to do her some type of bodily harm, she feared. Everyone was an assassin looking for her to exterminate her into oblivion. She was huddled up in a corner and her mind was racing away. She did not hear the nurse call her name, but with a wave of the nurse's arm, she rose and walked robotically into the doctor's office.

After her vital signs were taken and recorded on the flow sheet, Dr. D. came in. He saw her body language and knew immediately that she was in a highly anxious state of mind. He calmly settled in behind her, and the session began. He asked the same battery of questions and the repeat of answers until Dr. D. was bored. She was not responding to the evidenced-based therapy used across the board. Dr. D. thought to himself, *This is getting us nowhere fast.* He had to think outside the box, so he took the coin he found in his office out of his pocket and began an attempt to hypnotize her.

After a few minutes, he was successful in putting her into a deep sleep and led her down a road of suggestion. He asked her what she wanted to do in life and to be truthful. She stated that she wanted to be a police officer and work with juveniles found in the poverty-stricken area downtown. Johnny commanded her to go to the police station after her visit and apply for the police academy. He also told her to put him down for a reference and he would try to help her get into the police academy for new officers. He told her to be happy and content because she would be much happier soon after she pursues her dream.

Once the session was over, she no longer looked at others with feelings of paranoia and resentment. She concluded in her mind that people for the most part were kind and willing to try and understand so they could be understood. As always, Dr. D. ended the session by prescribing some anti anxiety medication along with his usual puzzle recommendation of the moment. She was to make a follow-up appointment at the first available slot.

Dr. S. was noticing how Dr. D. was working with the staff and the patients. He was very happy with the progress that they were making as a team and invited Dr. D. over to his house for dinner.

Dr. S. asked how many they could expect for dinner, and Dr. D. said he would be coming alone, but he would gladly accept his invitation and would be there at 6 p.m. this Saturday. Dr. S. was very pleased that he accepted his invitation and could not wait to tell his wife the good news. They were going to have a guest for dinner on Saturday at around 6:00 p.m.

Dr. D. walked home day after day which provided him good cardiovascular exercise and a routine that he had grown accustomed to. Once he got home, he would get an instant noodle soup container out and heat some water up in a pan. He would then mix the hot water with the soup and an instant dinner was served. After he ate his dinner, he would retire to his balcony, watch the squirrels run around in the trees, and the birds flying through the air. He would finish the evening going to sleep on the floor as he listened to the hustle and bustle of people that lived all around him. He fell asleep realizing how blessed he was to have a roof over his head and food in his stomach. His necessities were not always met in times past, but now he felt secure and safe for the moment.

CHAPTER 17

Dinner with the S.'s

Saturday came and off he went to Dr. S.'s home. The meal they served was more than he was accustomed to. A huge roast was served with mashed potatoes, gravy, and English peas. Dr. S. said the blessing and it was time to enjoy the food. The desert was cherry jubilee, and Dr. D. did his best to enjoy the meal, but he was not used to such huge portions. Mrs. S. asked Dr. D: "Does your meal look good?"

"Yes, the meal looks great. Thank you, Dr. and Mrs. S., for the invite, and the meal tasted just as good as it looked." Mrs. S. smiled with pride and squeezed her husband's hand in a way that he knew she was happy with his new partner. After dinner the two doctors retired to the piano room for coffee, cigars, and brandy. A baby grand piano was centered in the room and looked as though it had not been played for some time. Dr. D. had learned how to play the piano at the orphanage, and he enjoyed playing if he had a willing audience. Mrs. S. encouraged him to play a tune on the dusty instrument. Dr. D. played a Mozart song called the "Turkish March" that was popular during its time, and they enjoyed every note he played.

Mrs. S. hoped her husband would bring him around again sometime soon. Dr. S. had mentioned that Dr. D. wore the same clothes to the clinic every day, so Mrs. S. took the liberty of providing Dr. D. with some clothes that her husband had outgrown and a hot plate for later on that night. She was an excellent hostess and had studied hard in the school of southern hospitality. Dr. D. said goodnight and enjoyed his brisk walk home.

Time was moving along for Dr. D. as he was teaching school, helping in the clinic, or performing research on the homeless people in the area. He had lost all sense of who he really was and took on the doctor's identity completely with no hallucinations.

Dr. S. was wondering about Dr. D.'s credentials and why they had taken so long to get to the U.S. The doctor had been at the clinic for two months, and it was time to get the credentials, establish a medical number, and transfer his license to the American Board of Psychiatry and Neurology. Joint Commission (a governing agency that credentials medical institutions in the U.S.) would need these credentials for the clinic to stay accredited. Being accredited with this entity usually is associated with being successful in medicine or not. Dr. S. was beginning to wonder if his new partner was truly a doctor, or if he was someone else. Dr. S. tried to block out any suspicion that he had because the patients were in need of care, and he had to devote his efforts to them.

Dr. S.'s Interesting Patient

Dr. S. had an interesting case come into his office on this particular day. He considered bringing Dr. D. in to observe how he approached the situation, and so the two of them waited for his next patient. Dr. S. introduced himself to the young lady and sat as usual behind her and began to listen to her chief complaint. She began the session by admitting that she was addicted to sex. Dr. S. was taken back at first, but after refocusing, he told her to please continue. She said she had loved many men and could not seem to help herself. She would fantasize even when she was by herself and would self-fulfill her own needs when she could not get satisfied any other way. She explained how many ways she could have sex, but the most incredible climax came when one of her partners began to choke her.

She said, "At first it was lightly performed, but I wanted him to squeeze my throat tighter. He was on me performing well, choking me until I was on the verge of passing out, and then I climaxed multiple times during the sexual intercourse. It was something beautiful to behold, and I have tried to get my other partners to choke me, but so far, he is the only one that will do it."

Dr. S. took his handkerchief and wiped the sweat off his face. Dr. S. and Dr. D. were having a hard time refocusing on the lady's problem after her in-depth explanation. Dr. D. finally stepped up and asked Dr. S. if he could continue the session. Dr. S. said that it was alright with him if it was ok with the patient. After the patient agreed to the swap, Dr. D. asked her if she had ever been hypnotized for her addiction.

"No, I have not," she stated.

Dr. D. pulled the chain with the coin out and swung it in front of her face and said, "You are getting sleepy; your eyes are having a hard time staying open; you are getting very sleepy, and you can only respond to my voice." Dr. D. asked her if she could hear him and only him. She came back and said that she could, and he began his hypnotic suggestion therapy. Dr. D. asked her to think about all the times she had sex and how satisfied she was right after the act. "Now, from this moment on, I want you to be physically satisfied as if you have just had sex by swimming laps intensely at a local pool. Read *The Beginners Guide to Swimming* to help you get started and to help you stay away from casual sex with multiple partners. Ok, now when I count to three, I will snap my fingers, and I want you to wake up feeling great. You will not remember this conversation, but you will remember what I said subconsciously. One, two, and three. Wake up!"

The patient woke up and smiled at Dr. D. He wrote her a prescription for some placebo anti-sex medicine, told her to get an over-the-counter hot water bottle, and to flush her vagina out once a day. He wanted her to make a follow up appointment in a month to review her progress. She smiled and walked to the front desk to schedule her next session. Dr. S. was impressed with Dr. D. 's work and told him so.

CHAPTER 19

Dogs, Chicken Bones, and ACLS

As they stood in the doorway that separated the office from the waiting room, they noticed a small group of people eating fried chicken from a local restaurant. The oldest man in the group was Dr. S.'s patient. As Dr. S. got closer, he shook hands with the client and invited him into his office. The gentleman began choking on a chicken bone. Dr. S. was unaware of the crisis, and the man grabbed Dr. S. around the throat and started choking him. Just as Dr. S. was about to lose consciousness, Dr. D. moved in quickly and punched the man in the belly as hard as he could. He did not know what else to do in the current situation. The man let go of Dr. S., and the chicken bone popped out of his throat like a projectile missile due to the blow. It flew across the room and buried itself in the hair of a female patient waiting for her appointment.

Another patient in the waiting room had brought in their feisty little dog by saying they were blind, and it was their seeing eye dog. It was supposed to be well-mannered and assist the patient with their disability. As soon as the chicken bone hit the lady's hair, the Chihuahua jumped up on top of a table beside the lady and grabbed the chicken bone. Once he had the bone in his jaws, he ran around the room several times, smiling at everyone. Everyone was chasing the dog, and the owner fainted as her dog avoided being subdued. He finally made his grand exit by jumping out of an open window, while the patients in the waiting room pondered what had just taken place.

Everything had happened so fast, and Dr. D. was still standing in a boxer's stance to protect his partner, eventually realizing that the crisis was over. He tried to relax but knew something was still wrong with the situation. He heard the nurse scream that Dr. S. was not responding, not breathing, and had no pulse. Dr. D. told the nurse to get on the phone and call 911 or 0 for help. Dr. D. was once again in a stressful situation with someone who he felt was not only a colleague but a friend as well. On one hand he had accidentally saved the life of a patient in the waiting room, but on the other hand he was faced with reviving the chief of the psychology department on his own. He was relying on what he could remember from the asylum where he had been instructed on CPR, and a recent instruction class given to the medical school students about advanced cardiac life support (ACLS), which he was required to attend.

He felt for Dr. S's pulse, praying that he would feel something. The only thing he felt was his cold, blue, and placid skin. He knew he had to start CPR immediately if Dr. S. was to have any chance at all for survival. So, he gave two breaths and gave thirty chest compressions deep and fast. He repeated this sequence until the nurse stepped in to assist him with a two-person CPR technique. During the sequence of chest compressions and manual breaths, someone had brought the emergency box to the scene. It contained airway adjuncts, EKG pads, equipment for intubation, a heart monitor with defibrillation capability, and medications for sudden death cardiac events. It was opened and the EKG pads were put in place for an immediate rhythm check.

Dr. D. commanded that all personnel were to stand clear while he reviewed the heart rhythm as the machine recorded it. Dr. D. was so full of adrenaline that he was pushing the chest down a good two-and-a-half inches and blowing a good mouthful of air into Dr. S.'s lungs. After about seven complete cycles of high-quality CPR, the paramedics arrived and took over. They rushed Dr. S. to the university hospital and took him straight to the emergency room. Dr. D. was so distraught that he just sat down for a moment in the waiting room at the clinic, closed his eyes, and said a quick prayer for Dr. S. "Please, Lord, do not let Dr. S. My friend, die."

Dr. D. then got up and took care of every patient still waiting in the clinic. Once his clinic hours were over, Dr. D. went straight over to the hospital to see if Dr. S. had pulled through, been admitted, and if he was ok. Dr. S. was admitted for overnight observation, and when he saw Dr. D., he hugged his neck and said, "Thank you for saving my life." Dr. D. sat down in a recliner, had a wonderful visit with his partner, and felt an even closer connection with Dr. S. Johnny had reassured Dr. S. and himself of his capabilities through his actions. He would have a job at the clinic, if he desired to stay with them, for as long as he wanted. Dr. D. had to tell someone of his experience in the clinic. He went to class where he saw Tammy and tried to tell her what all had taken place, but he was so shy all he could do was look at her and look quickly away when she looked back. He said to himself that today would be different.

CHAPTER 20

Dr. D. and Tammy

They had been working together for about three months now, and he could feel the chemistry between them. Both were shy and inexperienced at dating. Tammy had classes that occupied most of her time, and Johnny had his illness that kept him from experiencing any type of close relationships of the opposite sex. Tammy was strangely drawn to Dr. D. and wanted to go out with him and get to know him better. Dr. D. felt the same way and was working on getting up his courage to ask her out for something besides a cup of coffee.

Dr. D. came up to Tammy after class and asked her out to dinner Saturday if she was not busy. A long pause that seemed like forever came over the room. Dr. D. thought he would pass out right there on the spot, but Tammy interrupted his thought with a riveting yes. She accepted the date and ran home after class to think about what had just happened. She was surprised that he asked her and even more surprised that she said yes. How was she going to fit this date into her busy schedule? After all, she had some of her hardest classes to get through, and she had Dr. D.'s class to assist with.

Saturday came and Dr. D. showed up with no car, no flowers, or presents of any type. He was just his usual self with a black suit, white shirt, black tie, and black dress shoes. Tammy thought that this was different but interesting. She was impressed with his straightforward approach to dating, and Johnny was impressed with how amazing she looked. Her hair was lying on her shoulders with some curl, she had on a pair of white pants that complimented her figure, and her navy blue blouse was opened in the front to magnify her cleavage. She stepped out onto the porch, down the steps, and went out to the sidewalk for their stroll to the restaurant.

Dr. D. could not help but to stare because of her sexy and stunning appearance. Eventually, Dr. D. got up the nerve to hold Tammy's hand. She pulled away at first and he apologized for his forward boldness. They got to the Greek restaurant and had a good dinner with all the trimmings. He told her what he had experienced at the clinic. At first it caused her great concern, thinking about the scenario that had occurred. She was impressed with his medical skills and held onto every word as he continued to tell her what had happened. She was glad that everyone was ok and began to tell him how the class was doing. She also gave him some names of the students who needed a little extra help throughout the semester.

As a TA she was not allowed to assist students in the upper-level classes, but Dr. D. had allowed her to run the class as she saw fit. She graded papers, made assignments, and gave lectures. Dr. D. was there to oversee the daily class operation when it was necessary. Tammy had appreciated the level of autonomy and confidence Dr. D. had given her as a TA at the university.

After dinner Dr. D. was allowed to hold Tammy's hand as they walked and talked, strolling down the street getting closer to her house. She still lived with her parents and saw no reason to leave until she got married or was able to secure a good job after graduation. Dr. D. was wondering how he could be having such a good conversation with an incredible woman such as Tammy. She was more than just a friend, and he desired to get even closer to her than he ever dared before.

As they reached her front doorstep, he spun her around and gave her a very slow and longing kiss. Tammy, not expecting such a move, gritted her teeth and said she did not do that. She pushed him away and ran into the house a little afraid but even more frustrated. Dr. D. somewhat surprised at the response just quietly turned around and walked away. He thought to himself that he would never take her out again. Neither one of them would forget this day for the rest of their lives. Tammy wanted to be with Dr. D. but was afraid to be comfortable around him. Dr. D. had strong feelings for Tammy but knew he had too many secrets that could not be revealed at this point in their relationship.

The class was awkward, and the students could feel the tension between Dr. D. and Tammy. After a couple of weeks, Dr. D. asked Tammy out to the movies where he hoped to discuss what happened and to apologize for his abrupt behavior. Saturday night came and Dr. D. met Tammy at her door with some flowers and a box of candy. A big smile came to Tammy's face that made her glow radiantly in the night. Once they took their seats in the movie house, Dr. D. began to apologize for his forwardness on their previous date.

Out of nowhere Tammy reached over and kissed Dr. D. passionately, which caused Dr. D. to lose his train of thought. After the kiss Tammy realized how good they were together and hoped that they could continue to see one another on a more intimate level. Dr. D. also noted how excited Tammy had gotten with just one kiss. The heavy breathing and perspiring had just gotten started. Tammy knew instinctively from that kiss that they could make a real couple.

As they continued to wrestle around passionately in the back of the movie house seats, his hands found their way to her breasts and thighs. He was clumsy but she did not care; it just felt good. After this date it became an every Saturday night thing between Tammy and Dr. D. He was quite excited to have a relationship with the opposite sex and wondered if it might lead to marriage, children, and happiness with a future. Johnny had forgotten for a moment that he had some serious issues of his own and needed to come clean if he wanted to have a chance with Tammy.

Getting back to the clinic, Dr. D. had little time to daydream or ponder these things about his newfound love because he was the only doctor at the clinic. He was busy seeing all the patients in the clinic. His favorite therapy was found in hypnosis, which he had somehow perfected by this point. Not only was he able to break down barriers, but he could find out what initially caused the barriers, which allowed him to make suggestions that could help patients overcome future barriers. Although he used the flashy coin left by the psychiatrist before him, he developed and used other forms of hypnosis to meet the patients' needs. Dr. D. got so wrapped up in his new life that he had forgotten that he was a schizophrenic and in need of psychiatric care himself. Every patient who came into the clinic saw Dr. D. who used hypnosis and other therapy founded on evidence-based research to help them have a better quality of life.

CHAPTER 21

Tommy's Problem

A couple of months went by when a very interesting case came into the clinic. His name was Tommy. A young man of approximately twenty-nine years of age who looked like something out of a Viking novel. He was seeking help with his continued fight against depression and aggression. Tommy was about six feet, six inches tall and weighed close to three hundred pounds of solid muscle. He had been in the army and was assigned to the Airborne Ranger's squad.

While under hypnosis Dr. D. was able to discover that the young man's wife could not reach an orgasm while they were having sex. This troubled the young man and made him paranoid that she was cheating on him, which caused him to have depressive episodes. This also made him impotent at times, and they could not enjoy being with each other intimately. While Tommy was still under hypnosis, Dr. D. suggested that the next time he and his wife had sex, after five minutes, he should lightly choke his wife until she had an orgasm. If she passed out, he should let go of her throat and watch her closely to make sure she recovered. After all, it had worked for the sex addict who had visited the clinic earlier, and maybe it would help Tommy with his marriage problems pertaining to sexual intercourse.

After waking Tommy up, he prescribed some antidepressants and a 1000-piece puzzle to be completed before their next session. Tommy was escorted by Dr. D. to the exit door, and Dr. D. gave him his cell phone number to call him any time day or night if he needed anything. Tommy shook hands with the doctor, and they went their separate ways. Dr. D. did not give it much thought and continued his work, seeing patient after patient in the clinic.

CHAPTER 22

The Nurse and ECT

The next clinic day he had an appointment with a nurse who was suffering from depression. She had not been able to eat or go outside her home for two weeks and was a nervous wreck at the time of her appointment. Dr. D. had talked with her, and she wanted to have electroconvulsive shock therapy (ECT) to end her depressive state of being. After giving her all the reasons he could think of why she should not go through with it, he finally submitted to her desire, and off to the ECT lab they went. The benefits outweighed the risks in her special case, and once the patient was in the room, an IV was started and some fluids were attached to keep her vein open so medications could be given throughout the procedure. Conscious sedation was used when ECT was given at this time. It would be a more comfortable experience with the drugs on board.

Although the patient would still experience a grand mal seizure, the intensity would be less severe. The nurse did everything that Dr. D. ordered, and he explained to the patient everything that was going to happen so there would be no surprises. The patient told him to just give her the therapy, this was not her first rodeo, and everything would be just fine. Dr. D. walked over to the ECT device and pressed the button that delivered the shock. It was a terrifying site to see the seizure and the limp body afterward. It reminded Dr. D. of some of the things he had witnessed in the asylums during his stay and how he swore he would never go back to one. Dr. D. left the ECT room and walked down the hall to his office where he could not quit thinking about the smell of burning flesh and the awkward appearance of the acute seizure.

CHAPTER 23

ECT, Hypnosis, and the Homeless Mentally Ill

Somewhere throughout his day he had an epiphany. Why not give the homeless mentally ill patients a slight shock of ECT and immediately hypnotize them, suggesting a new perspective, history, and a purpose of life? He could rewrite the script that some of his friends had been dealt. It sounded really good, and he was anxious to try it on some of the homeless that he and Dr. S. were working at the clinic.

A couple of days went by, and Dr. D. had worked up an angle for getting the homeless mentally ill to sign waivers so he could experiment on them. His first subject agreed to the experiment and signed all the paperwork necessary for it to be legal and documented. He sat down with the subject and explained every pro and con of the experiment. After all of the legal documentation was performed, Dr. D. and the medical staff began to prepare the patient for ECT.

After the procedure Dr. D. hypnotized him with his favorite coin on a chain. He instilled moral, ethical, and practical values into the mind of the subject. The ECT had done its job and wiped out all the patient's memories. Dr. D. was then able to replace it with things that would help him assimilate into society. It was a drastic step but the theory behind the therapy was sound. Dr. D. called in the case worker to follow up on the subject and to assist him with job placement and housing until he could do it on his own.

CHAPTER 24

The Loss of Johnny B.

As Johnny continued to grow into his new role, he was beginning to lose his own person and was slowly becoming the imposter he had created. Days became weeks, weeks became months, and months became years. Before Johnny knew it, he was engaged and a senior partner at the clinic. Everything was going great, and he had reached a point in his life where he was beginning to feel accomplished. Tammy was his bright spot just on the horizon, and everything was falling into place. His students were able to pass their boards, and his patients were getting well or at least well enough to function in society. For Dr. D. Johnny was just a bad dream, and he was now and always going to be Dr. D. He had just walked Tammy home after a movie as was their custom on Saturday nights. He returned to his home and walked in the door to relax for a little while before going to bed. He went over the events of the evening in his mind when all of a sudden he received a phone call from a patient who was frantic.

CHAPTER 25

The Crisis

It was Tommy and he could not explain what had happened over the phone but just continued to say he needed him to come over to his house immediately. Dr. D. had forgotten about this patient because it had been a while since he had been to the clinic. Tommy gave Dr. D. his address and begged him to hurry. Dr. D. was trying to gather his thoughts, and he quickly called for a taxi to get to his patient as quickly as possible.

Once Dr. D. had arrived at the address provided, he saw Tommy pacing up and down the front porch with a wild look on his face. It hit Dr. D. immediately and he began to recollect the appointment. He recalled that this was the man who had trouble with his wife in the bedroom and she could not get satisfied with her husband Tommy. Dr. D. remembered the prescribed therapy and began to feel a sudden sense of despair. Dr. D. went up onto the porch and approached Tommy to find out what the problem was. Tommy began telling Dr. D. that for some unknown reason when he and his wife made love, he would start to choke her, and this usually led to her being able to achieve an orgasm.

"Tonight, we were in the middle of our lovemaking, and it was going great, but I had to choke her a little longer than usual to help her reach her climax. For some strange reason I could not quit choking her until she passed out, and I think I have killed her." Dr. D was in shock and wanted to run away but knew that was not the answer. He had put these thoughts into this young man's mind, and if he had committed murder, it would be the end of his practice, future, and life. Dr. D. asked Tommy if he could examine the body, and Tommy agreed as he escorted him into the bedroom where the body was. She was a beautiful young lady, naked, and lifeless on the bed where her husband had left her. Dr. D. told Tommy to call 911 or 0 and the police immediately before something else happened.

Dr. D. stayed beside Tommy while they waited for the ambulance and the police. Tommy was confused and asked Dr. D., "What am I going to tell the paramedics and the police when they get here?" Dr. D. said to tell them the truth, and he would stand with him throughout the whole process. Tommy explained to both the paramedics and the police what had taken place and how he had accidentally choked the life out of his wife while engaged in sexual intercourse. As the police started to form a conclusion and take down a statement, Dr. D. stepped up and said that he would go with Tommy to the hospital with his wife in the ambulance if that was permissible. Once they arrived at the facility, they could gather more information and take down his statement at that time. He further explained that Tommy was a patient of his at the clinic who suffered from depression and had been under his direct supervision over the past couple of years. The officers agreed to the request, and everyone made their way to the hospital.

Tommy went in the ambulance with his wife to the ER, and Dr. D. subtly slid out the back door of the hospital once he saw that they had arrived safely. He ran all the way home without stopping.

Dr. D. grabbed all the money he had stashed away in his bottom drawer and out the back door he went. He began to feel dizzy, and as he walked down the street, everything faded into darkness, but he felt as though he was still moving down the road. He was sleepwalking and did not have a clue where he was or where he was going. He was so stressed out about these recent events that he was going into a mental state he had never visited before. He was on his way to a new destination, unknown except in his own mind's eye, which was propelling him on blindly.

Back at the hospital, Tommy's wife had not died but only had passed out during their love making, and she woke up in the hospital. All her vital signs were perfect, and she hugged her husband's neck with a big grateful smile. The hospital discharged her without any questions. The police gave them a ride home, and Tommy and his wife had a long conversation about what had occurred. They concluded that when they were having relations, they needed to be more careful about the choking part, but the benefit outweigh the risk. They were once again the happy couple, and Tommy was very grateful to Dr. D. for standing beside him throughout this trying time in his life.

The next day Tommy went to the clinic to tell Dr. D. the good news about his wife and to bring the staff a box of donuts. When Tommy got to the clinic, Dr. D. had not arrived yet. It was unlike him to be late, and some of the staff were a little more than concerned. Dr. S. decided he was going to walk over to the house where Dr. D. lived and check on him. When he got to the home, no one was there, but the door was open, so he walked in to investigate. "Hello, is anyone home?" exclaimed Dr. S. in a loud voice to be heard throughout the house. No one answered, so he continued to examine the home and found a bed that had not been slept in, a closet full of unmolested clothes, but his partner was nowhere to be found. Dr. S. began to let his imagination get the best of him, and he called the police for assistance with locating his partner.

He waited for the police to show up, and they explained that in such cases they require the missing person to be missing for at least twenty-four hours before they could start to look for them. The doctor argued that this was absurd, and he needed his partner found immediately or he would take it up with the chief of police. After arguing with the officers, Dr. S. gave up and went to the clinic. The work was exhausting, and he missed his partner who was able to help him with the clinic. During his lunch break, Dr. S. went downtown to the police station in hope of getting something done about his friend who had been missing for six hours. He stepped into the entrance of the station and demanded to see the chief. He was escorted upstairs to a large office with a small-framed man inside.

The chief had thick black hair, wrinkly face, half-smoked cigar in his mouth, and a big pistol on his hip. He was resting in a thickly padded chair, teetering between consciousness, but still took the time to ask the doctor how he could be of service. Dr. S. began to explain what his concerns were. His partner has been missing now for six hours and something needed to be done right away. The chief leaned back in his chair and told the doctor that he could file a missing person's report after his friend has been missing for twenty-four hours. That was the policy, and he could read it for himself in the policy and procedure manual if he desired. Dr. S. finally saw that this was a waste of time and he excused himself from the conversation.

Discouraged and exhausted, he went back to the clinic, and he was able to treat the rest of the patients in the waiting room. The twenty-four-hour time frame evolved slowly but surely, and a full investigation was initiated. The police went back to where the doctor was last seen. It was with Tommy, and the police officers who had answered the call when Tommy's wife had her misfortune were the same ones who were attempting to backtrack Dr. D.'s path. When Tommy heard that the doctor was missing, he was overcome with sadness. He was more than Tommy's doctor; he was his friend as well. He joined the search, and together they searched all over Mobile, Alabama.

They searched outside the state, into Florida, Mississippi, and the lower part of Louisiana to no avail. The doctor had seemed to have vanished into thin air. Dr. S. had to break the news to the class that Dr. D. was teaching, and when Tammy heard the news, she fainted right on the spot. The class explained to Dr. S. that Tammy and Dr. D. had become engaged and were just waiting for the summer break to get married. Tammy was fearful that Dr. D. must have had some sort of accident or one of his patients might have taken him captive or worse. No one knew what had become of the good doctor who had done so much good not only for the clinic patients, students, but also for the homeless mentally ill. With no body and no motive, the search ended after a few months. Dr. S. posted a reward for his safe return and continued the search with Tammy, hoping to produce some answers. Also, the police put out an all-points bulletin seeking Dr. D.'s whereabouts for the closure of all stakeholders involved. The staff and the student body were on full alert and seeking the doctor. Sadly, he was nowhere to be found within the extended area of search.

CHAPTER 26

Dr. D. Takes on a New Role

Our main character, Dr. D., was exhausted and on the run. When he finally came out of his unconscious state of mind, he found himself in an unfamiliar place. He had no idea who he was or where he had come from. The stress from the chain of events that previously defined his life had taken its toll on Dr. D., and he was totally exhausted. He laid down on a park bench in front of a building and went to sleep. After a few hours of restless sleep, he was awakened due to the probing of a police officer's billy club.

"Hey, buddy, you can't sleep here," exclaimed the officer. "Who are you, do you have any identification, do you have any money? You look tired, broke, and hungry, so why don't you come down to the police station where we can rustle you up with something to eat and we can try and find out what happened to you. We also have some nice beds there that are a lot better than these park benches. I can provide you three hot meals and a cot until we can come up with a better alternative." Dr. D. agreed to go with the police officer and was able to get a good meal at the station.

Texas is proud of their barbecue, and this is what the officer gave Dr. D. that evening. The officer was curious about the man he found on the park bench. The man with no identification or money was found lying around on the street benches with bruises and lacerations about his head, arms, and chest. He attempted to take his fingerprints, but they were so traumatized with road rash or some other form of injury to his hands that the prints were illegible. Earlier that day Dr. D., during his amnesia episode, had stumbled on to a gang of young men on the south side of town who robbed him, beat him severely, and left him for dead.

The officer called the sheriff and provided Dr. D. with a bath, clean clothes, boots, and a hot meal per the sheriff's instruction. Dr. D. was put in a cell and fell asleep for two days, awaking only to relieve himself and to eat the meals provided, which were very good. What an unlucky break for Dr. D. who was unaware of who he was, placed in jail, robbed of his money, and lost all his identification papers. The sheriff showed up early one morning after Dr. D. had been with them for a month and told him that he had to be placed in the John Doe category of missing persons. Dr. D. felt like that name might be familiar: John. But not really understanding what that meant to him at the time, he continued to eat his breakfast while looking at the sheriff.

He reminded the sheriff of a wild animal which would not take their eyes off a predator when there was a confrontation. The sheriff was a tall, lean man and looked to be in his prime. He owned a cattle ranch just outside Lake Conroe in the northern part of Houston, Texas, and always was looking for new talent for his ranch. He wanted to help this John Doe and offered him a job on the ranch as a handyman, roustabout, and cowboy. He offered him one hundred dollars a week with room and board and a percentage of the end of the year cattle sales at auction. This was more than fair at the time, and it would be a win-win for both of them if Dr. D. accepted his offer. Dr. D. agreed to the job and could hardly sleep that night because of the excitement he felt of receiving employment with a possible future, but who was he before and why did this happen to him? Somehow, he had it in his mind that he always wanted to be a cowboy, and now he would have the opportunity. He would take the lemons that he was given, and he was going to make some lemonade.

CHAPTER 27

The Ranch is Boss, Hoss

The next morning an older, more experienced cowhand was sent over to fetch Dr. D. from the jail in an old ford pickup truck. Dr. D. walked out into the sunshine, climbed into the cab of the truck, and off to the ranch they went. This cowhand was the foreman on the ranch and his name was JD. He told Dr. D. that he had to have a name on the ranch so there would be no confusion on who he was addressing. Also, it would be a good idea in case of an emergency or some other serious situation. JD gave Dr. D. the name Tex and it stuck to him like mud. Dr. D. really liked his new name, especially since he could not remember any other one. He really did not have any choice in the matter and so Tex it was.

So now Johnny had become Dr. D. and Dr. D. had become Tex, just like that. So down the highway they rode and rode and rode in the old truck as it was clanging away. Just like a lot of places in Texas, when someone says something is right down the street it could be fifty miles away. Tex searched the old truck curiously with glancing eyes, because it was in his nature to be curious, and he found an old cowboy hat behind the seat of the truck. The hat was a true Stetson, and it was a perfect fit. JD just grinned and said,

"Well, Tex, that hat sure makes you look like a real cowboy, but let's see if you can earn your spurs on the ranch."

It took them about two hours to get to the ranch, but when they arrived, it was breathtaking. Not only was it acres and acres of land, but the homestead was totally self-contained with an endless supply of water from a well, milk, beef, and the chickens provided the eggs. An underground gas pocket and windmills that turned continuously gave the power supply that ran all the appliances. JD hopped down from the truck and introduced Tex to the rest of the guys at the bunkhouse. All the hands were excited to get another cowhand on the ranch because working shorthanded was zero fun and taking a toll on their morale. They were also curious about the newcomer who had no recollection of who he was or where he came from. "Complete and total amnesia" one of the fellows called it, but it was not contagious, he added.

JD told Tex he needed to get started right away, and he intro-duced him to Lefty who would show him the ropes on what needed to be done immediately. JD also told Tex not to hesitate to come to him if he needed anything. JD's motto was, "We are going to set you up for success, kid, and when you succeed, we all benefit." JD walked over to his horse and patted him on the head with a big smile. He asked his horse if he had missed him. Then he put his gun belt on and saddled up tall in his stirrups. JD started yelling at the rest of the crew, as his horse pranced around the men. He told them. "Let's get things rolling." So shortly after JD and Tex arrived, everyone was out rounding up strays and ushering the herd over to better feeding pastures.

Tex liked his new job and surroundings, and his first job was to fix the leak on the bunkhouse roof. He climbed up the ladder with Lefty, and together they were able to place a few new wooden shingles along with some tar in the area where the rain was seeping through.. It was easily spotted due to the change in the color of the wood on the roof. Cedar shakes were still being used in Texas and parts of California at the time. They were small, cheap, and easily replaced with just a few nails. The only drawback was that they were highly flammable when dried out, and this could be hazardous to everyone if they caught on fire. They were aesthetically pleasing and had a wonderful odor to counter the cow smell that hung in the air, especially in the summer. This is what was used on the roof of the bunkhouse and home at the sheriff's ranch, and it had been passed down from generation to generation without any incident. If the sheriff was ever questioned about the roof, he would always laugh and say, "If it is not broken, I am not going to fix it."

Tex was settling into his new role and found his bunk at the front of the beds on the right side. There was a set of chests of drawers for each cowhand to use during his stay at the ranch, and Tex found the setup satisfactory for his present situation. At the end of the day, he could hear the dinner bell ringing, and he followed all the other hands into the main house for dinner. The sheriff sat at the head of the table and JD sat at his right hand. The sheriff said grace, and a young lady was found standing beside her father at the head of the table. They were very close because she was his only child. He wanted to make sure he left everything to her and that she would be able to handle anything that came down the pike.

Her mother had died young from a seven-foot rattler that bit her when she was out in the field chasing some of the strays back into the gates. A lot of the cowboys remembered her and said that her daughter was the spitting image of her mother. Tex thought she was the most beautiful woman in the world, and she caught him staring at her a couple of times during the evening supper, which aroused her curiosity. Everybody on the ranch had a job to perform, and the sheriff's daughter was no exception. Her duties included but were not limited to serving as a cook, butler when necessary, and a maid.

She had long, wavy jet-black hair, a nice tan, big brown eyes, and a set of white teeth that could be seen a mile away. She was sturdy and smart as a whip. She had just graduated high school and was in her first year of college. She was majoring in agriculture, so she was wanting to transfer to Texas A&M after completing her first two years at the nearby junior college in order to save money and to be close to her father. If she could finish at the junior college with high scores, she would earn a scholarship, finish at Texas A&M, and help her father with the ranch after graduation. The only thing standing in her way was her hormones, which had been working overtime, and she could not stop thinking about the opposite sex. She was looking Tex over with a discerning eye and decided to hang out with him a little while after dinner. She wanted to get to know this cowpoke a little better, and he was not so bad to look at.

After the wonderful meal, the sheriff's daughter came out on the porch and found Tex out there looking up at the stars. She introduced herself as Suzie, and he was able to stutter out that his name was T-T-T-T-Tex. Suzie could not contain her laughter, which caused Tex to become even more red-faced than the Texas sun had already made him. She asked him where he came from and what he thought of her father's ranch. Tex just listened and thought to himself how lucky he was to be walking in the Texas moonlight with such a beautiful, charming, and nice girl. They got along so well; she talked and walked as he listened to her every word. Tex did not talk much, and that was all right with Suzie because she liked to talk.

Eventually, she told him that it was getting late, and she had to go in and clean up before bed, but she enjoyed their walk, and they would have to do it again sometime. Tex just shook his head up and down in a yes motion and off she went into the big house. Tex walked over to the bunkhouse and found everyone already asleep, so he tiptoed in, crawled into his bunk, and soon he was joining them in a restful sleep.

About 4 a.m. the breakfast bell rang, and all the hands got up and lined up for breakfast. An egg and some bacon were sandwiched in a biscuit for each cowboy. A cup of coffee was provided to wash it down with. Afterward, Tex was met by Lefty, and he was handed a branding iron. Lefty said, "We got to get the brand on those cows before they have a chance to fully wake up and disappear."

Tex said, "Let's go," and off they went, heating up the iron and branding the cows for placement in the herd. After they finished with the cows, it was time to feed the horses and clean their stalls. Once this chore was completed, the sun was coming up and they sat down for a coffee break. It was fall and the Texas plains were not getting hot like they did in the summer, so all the cowhands were enjoying the cooler weather. Lefty noticed how tanned Tex had become in just the few weeks he had been at the ranch. He reaffirmed that every summer that Texas heat would come back on them with a vengeance.

During the first week of Tex's stay, Suzie had noticed that he was in pain from the sunburn and was starting to develop a plan on how to help the newcomer, who would need some help against that harsh Texas sun in the summer. She had a nice garden full of all kinds of herbs, which she was able to make into remedies for the cowboys. They were miles away from town, and without her help, some hands would have been out of luck and possibly would have died. She was already a good herbal medicine healer with a tender touch and in-depth knowledge of plants and their impact on health.

CHAPTER 28

Cowboy Up, Tex

Tex and Lefty went back to work mending fences on the edge of the property. On the north side of the property, they noticed a small group of cattle had made their way through the fence and were headed towards the highway. Lefty told Tex to go to the stable and round up a couple of horses so he could show him how to retrieve the small herd. Tex ran all the way to the stables and got two horses for the redirection of the cows. He put saddles on their backs, bridles in their mouths, and ran them over to where he had left Lefty. They both mounted the horses and, copying Lefty's movements, Tex grabbed his lariat and began to hit the side of his horse's thigh. He was yelling at the cows and herding them back into the fence just like Lefty. He was a natural at this kind of work and he caught on fast.

Once each head of cattle was inside the fence, they had to work quickly to repair the fence before any of the cows decided they liked the graze better on the other side of the fence. Lefty really appreciated Tex's hard work and let him know it with a big Texas grin and a firm handshake. "Come on, Tex, let's get these doggies back with the rest of the herd." After working on the fences, it was time to check on the herd. Tex was riding a Mustang, and they seemed to get along just fine. The sheriff was glad to see Tex assimilate so well, but he still had the nagging question in the back of his mind, *Who is he, really?* Lefty, JD, and the rest of the cowboys just saw him as another hand who needed a job, and the sheriff did not tell them any different.

The sheriff's daughter was starting to take a little bit more interest in Tex and her mind would wander. She would often catch herself thinking about the stranger that was new to her world. Who was he, really? Every day at sundown the bell rang out for dinner to be served. All the cowboys washed their hands, and the sheriff would say grace before everyone would dig in. After a month, Tex began to be very thankful that he had found not only employment, but also friends to watch his back in many different circumstances.

CHAPTER 29

Suzie, Her Secret, and Tex

Suzie was daydreaming about Tex and felt like she needed to make the first move in the relationship. It was beginning to be spring-time in Texas and the days were getting longer. Suzie caught Tex walking around the ranch as was his custom after dinner and asked him to come with her for a walk in the woods; she had something she wanted to show him. As they walked, she talked a lot about the ranch, college, possibly starting a family, and her dad. Tex was an excellent listener and just walked and smiled as they strolled in the moonlight, just like all the previous times they had been together.

After a little while, Tex asked her if their destination was much farther. She laughed and said, "What's the matter, you're getting tired or something? You aren't scared, are you?"

Tex just tipped his hat and said, "Of course not, ma'am; just wondering where we are going." Tex added, "There is nothing out here worrying me except maybe you, good looking."

Suzie just blushed and she said with a start, "Here we are." Tex took off his old cowboy hat, looked around hard, but could not see what all the excitement was about. Suzie told him to follow her and stay close, "so you don't get lost." At a point under a marked tree that Suzie recognized, she stomped her cowgirl boot down into the earth, and a trapped door flipped up on one side, exposing a small tunnel. Down she went with Tex right behind her. They were so close to each other that Suzie could feel Tex's manhood against her buttocks down in the dark cave. She giggled excitedly, and Tex felt his growing enlargement in his jeans. He asked himself, *What is this crazy girl up to?*

After a few more steps, Suzie pushed up on the roof of the tunnel and it opened into a dark room. She had some generators set up on the sides of the walls of the room that were gas powered. She flipped a switch and the room lit up with a large group of beautiful plants spaced out exactly three feet apart. Tex did not understand what she was showing him, but Suzie, over the course of the winter had noticed some wonderful attributes about Tex, and she was falling in love with him. She did not want to hold any secrets from him, so she sat down with him to explain exactly what she was showing him.

She began the conversation with the pair of them sharing a cigarette she had hand rolled herself. Tex thought that this was awkward but went along with it, because over the course of the winter he had also fallen for Suzie. He thought how amazing she was, and she would make anyone an awesome wife. Suzie's eyes started to squint, and they were turning red. Tex did not know why this was happening but eventually he felt like it must be her brand of cigarettes. He noticed how they stunk up the room and how Suzie would start laughing. She would laugh so hard until she cried and then she got down to business.

"Ok, Tex, this is the deal. This is a hidden marijuana operation that was set up by some ex-military guys before my dad added this land to our ranch. He bought it but had no idea that this green house was right here under his nose. You can't see this operation, not even in the daytime, due to the covering of the trees and the camouflaged tent. Also, to get in, you have to know where the secret door is, and I alone have the key. The veterans that built this farm got a little nervous when they found out that the sheriff of the county was buying the land, so they took off and left their operation intact.

I found it a couple of years back by accident when I accidentally fell into the tunnel after the cows had wandered through the woods. One of them had set off the trap door, and it was exposed for a short period of time. I come out and check on the plants all the time and sit here to have a smoke and prune my bushes. It keeps them healthy, and I can grind up the buds, add a little hand lotion, and it becomes a topical anesthetic. I have used it for sore muscles, headaches, and around my private parts for an increase in my libido." Tex asked her if she was kidding, and she said that everything she had told him was the truth. Tex asked Suzie if she had some of that cream on her. Suzie said, "I do, but why do you want it, Tex?" Tex asked her to give him a sample. Suzie handed him a small amount of the cream and he applied it to his penis to see if it would work. Suzie laughed so hard she could not see straight, and Tex ran out of the tent screaming because his penis was on fire.

Tex ran all the way home and took a long, cold shower in the bunkhouse. The next day Suzie made Tex swear never to mention the tent or its whereabouts because she could get in a lot of trouble if it was ever discovered by the authorities. Tex and Suzie were spending a lot of nights going out to the tent, and although Suzie seemed to enjoy smoking that stinky tobacco, Tex did not see what the big deal was. Suzie explained to him that it was like the drinking that he and the other cowboys did when they went out to Gilley's on Saturday night. She also let him in on the fact that it would not give him a hangover the next day or make him sick to his stomach. Tex asked her if he could try that smoke one more time, and this time it hit him solid.

Suzie said that most of the time anyone who tries marijuana for the first time will not get that high feeling that it can provide. It usually takes a couple of times before it really gets into your system and makes you stoned. Tex started to better understand what Suzie was talking about as he spent more time with her in the tent getting high and just grooving with nature.

One night Suzie and Tex were in the tent, and after a few cigarettes, a thunderstorm blew in. They were enjoying each other's company, the thunder, the lightning, and the sound of the rain coming down on the roof of the tent. It was very warm and dry. Tex and Suzie laughed at the storm with great admiration. How forceful the lightning and thunder seemed and at times a little frightening. Tex closed his eyes and Suzie reached over to kiss him without any warning. She was young and had needs of her own. She was high on marijuana and so was Tex, which exacerbated their hormones. She was going to take full advantage of the situation, and so their lovemaking began.

Tex and Suzie were breathing so heavy you could see the steam rising off their naked bodies as they held on tight to one another. This was a moment that Suzie had been longing for, and now she was going to get it. She grabbed Tex's penis and started rubbing it on her thighs until she was so wet that the fluid was running down her leg. Tex was fully erected, and Suzie could not believe how big he was when she got a look at his manhood in the moonlight. She was so ready that she hoped on top of him, and his penis slid right in without any resistance. They both moaned, panted, and Suzie screamed as she came with great bursts of pleasure. She was able to take all of him deep inside of her and she was in extreme ecstasy.

Tex was enjoying himself as well but had seen the cows and horses mating with a position that was insertion from behind their mate. He had not yet achieved an orgasm and he wanted to make love using the example he had seen in nature. Suzie agreed and before he knew it, he was coming deep inside of Suzie, but to his surprise she had another orgasm at the same time. They both collapsed and laid beside each other with an interlude that lasted for a short period of time. They continued to talk, caress, and after the break they were in their positions for another session of lovemaking. It was like two boxers slugging it out and then the bell sounds for the end of round one. This kept up throughout the night, but eventually it was time to get back to the ranch and go to sleep.

Daybreak comes early and there is no time for staying out in the woods all night. The next evening after dinner, the two young adults headed back out to the tent for another secret rendezvous. They continued their meetings until it got extremely hot in the tent, and they were forced to try and make other plans. Suzie had a car, and she would meet Tex about a mile down the driveway for their secret getaway. Eventually, it was no secret, and the ranch was talking about the couple, which got back to the sheriff.

As the summer became fall again, the sheriff met Tex out by the road as he was waiting on Suzie. He asked if he could have a word and Tex agreed without any hesitation. The sheriff began the conversation and asked Tex if he was serious about his daughter. Tex asked him exactly what he meant. The sheriff asked him if he was in love with his daughter and if he planned on marrying her. This caught Tex off guard, and he stammered a little but came across with a resounding yes on all accounts. The sheriff grinned a big Texas grin, slapped Tex on the back, and said, "Welcome to the family, boy." The sheriff asked Tex what his last name was but remembered that Tex did not even know what his first name was. The sheriff asked him how he liked the name Tee. Tex said that would be fine with him and he would ask the sheriff's daughter to marry him that night.

CHAPTER 30

The Proposal, Wedding, and the Good Life

Suzie picked up Tex at the same rendezvous spot as usual. When they got to the drive-in movie, Tex got out of the car, got down on one knee, and proposed to Suzie right there on the spot. Suzie said yes and they were married in the church that spring. Friends and family were invited, and the church was bursting at the seams with all the guests. After the service, the sheriff handed an envelope to Tex with two tickets to Hawaii and five thousand dollars. Tex shook his hand and away he and Suzie went to the airport and destination Hawaii Kei Kei for their honeymoon.

It was an amazing honeymoon, and most of the time the young couple could be found in the bungalow making love. Sometimes they would take a break and go for a walk down the beach in the middle of the night, but most of the time they were exploring one another's bodies in the bedroom.

After their honeymoon the couple made their way back to the ranch, and it was business as usual. Suzie was making meals and cleaning the house. Tex had moved up in rank as a real cowboy with Lefty's help. The sheriff had been reluctant to post Tex on guard patrol, but now that he was part of the family, he gave him a Winchester rifle and put him to work guarding the cattle from predators. Coyotes, wolves, and mountain lions were the main concern, but the cowboys had to watch out for other ranch hands stealing their herd as well. The sheriff also issued Tex a pistol that he always carried on him, except when he went into town for staples.

All week the ranch was alive with the work that had to be done. Saturdays and Sundays were set aside for relaxing and going to church. Only a few hands had to watch over the herd, which was rotated to give everyone a break. Saturday nights the cowboys would head over to Pasadena and Gilley's for a night of entertainment. Tex was very surprised the first time he went to Gilley's with the crew and saw the sign: "leave all weapons on the bar." Of course, the management was good about returning everyone's property to them when they left, but they did not want someone causing a serious injury to a paying customer.

Gilley's was a fun place for Tex and Suzie to go to socialize with young adults. You could catch them there on Saturday night doing the Texas two-step or the Cotton-Eyed Joe across the sawdust dance floor with the rest of the crowd. Maybe even get a few rounds in sitting on the mechanical bull as it bounced around furiously to throw the rider off. The object of the game was to see who could stay on it the longest. Mattresses were lined up around the bull to keep everyone safe if they were thrown off.

Sunday mornings were set aside for Sunday school and church. The cowboys were not required to go, but it was highly suggested that they attend. Worship is big in Texas, and if a person chooses not to go then it is frowned upon by the community. Tex and Suzie enjoyed going to the local Baptist church with the gang. Afterward, it was time for a big meal with all the trimmings. Suzie would get a break from her chores, and the sheriff would usually take over on the grill for the main course. He would also hire someone to come in and help out with Suzie's chores. Life was good, and every Sunday evening after the meal Tex and Suzie would go to their secret place in the woods to be alone.

One Sunday Tex and Suzie were out there inside the tent and Tex asked Suzie about the heaven and hell concept that he found in his Bible. He said that the preacher made sure to emphasize the subject that if you don't get saved then you are headed for hell. Suzie said that it was not a hard thing to understand. She explained that in the Bible it says that the wages of sin is death and that if you confess with your mouth that Jesus is the son of God and ask him to forgive you for all your sins, he will. No man cometh to the father except through Jesus Christ our Lord and Savior who died on the cross for all of us. Suzie, feeling led by the Holy Ghost, explained to Tex that if he felt led to get saved, he should say the sinner's prayer and ask Jesus to forgive him of his sins and to live in his heart right out there in the tent. Tex needed a little more information, so Suzie tried to explain it the best way she knew how.

"I can tell you, Tex, what happened to me, but I think we should pray first so that God can move, and if you are led after our talk, you can ask Jesus to be your personal savior." Tex agreed and so they prayed and asked God for guidance in this matter. Suzie told Tex that when she was nine years old, she went to a camp sponsored by the church and one of the counselors explained to her how Jesus had died on the cross for all our sins. "All we have to do is ask him to come into our heart, wash us clean with his blood, and repent from our sins. I said this prayer and he forgave me for all my sins. I got baptized at the camp, and I have tried to live in a way that I feel would bring honor to him."

Tex felt the Spirit move in him, and he said he wanted to ask Jesus into his heart to cleanse him from all his sins so he would go to heaven when he died because hell sounded like an awful bad place to go. Tex got down on his knees and, with Suzie's help, prayed for Jesus to forgive him for all of his sins and to come into his heart to be his personal savior. When Tex looked up and saw Suzie, they were both in tears. They felt God's joy, peace, and love as he blessed their commitment as man and wife, making their home one that would honor him.

The next Sunday Tex went down the aisle at the church and told the preacher what had happened. Tex said that he wanted to follow the Lord with baptism. The preacher told everyone in the church that Tex had gotten saved, and they were going to set up a time for baptism next Sunday, "so don't be late." Time went on at the ranch and Suzie conceived for Tex a baby boy. Tex could not have been happier, and they named him Tex Jr. The sheriff was so excited that he passed out cigars to the staff at the ranch and to all of the staff at the police station.

Everything was moving along as it should, but once Suzie came home with Tex Jr., she told Tex they needed a place of their own. Tex talked to the sheriff about it, and the sheriff marked off an acre of land out where he noticed the couple taking their evening strolls. He told Tex that once the herd was sold at market there would be some down time to build them a house on the property. It would be a perfect location with the woods close by for shade, hiking, and hunting. Also, it would not be too far from the main house so he could come by and see his grandson when he could. Tex explained the idea to Suzie, and she agreed to it, but they would have to get rid of the pot tent. The cowboys could help them build their house and they could move in before the winter hit. The sheriff continued to look for Tex's identity, but he did not pursue it too hard now that he was family. Tex was helping with the ranch and the sheriff trusted him with all he owned.

CHAPTER 31

Shoot-out at the Piggly Wiggly

One day Suzie went shopping at the Piggly Wiggly grocery store and Tex came in to check on her. He caught her over at the meat department and snuck up behind her, which made her jump. They both laughed and hugged each other tight. They kissed and she began telling him about her day. She asked him what they were going to have for supper. It was just like the walks they used to go on where she would talk and he listened. They made the perfect pair and life was good.

As they continued to catch up on their daily activities, they heard a loud skirmish in the front of the store. Two masked men were holding up the store and had guns on the manager who was on his knees trying to open up the safe. Tex and Suzie had startled the robbers which caused them to turn and shoot at the couple. Tex jumped in front of Suzie and knocked her to the ground. He then pulled out his revolver which he had accidentally carried to the store with him that day and fired back at the intruders, who were surprised and desperately trying to get away.

People screaming, money flying in the air, Tex chased after the criminals, and was able to shoot out the back right tire. He was a good shot with his six-shooter, and the bandits were lucky to get away alive. The robbers had spent more time than they wanted to at the Piggly Wiggly, and this allowed the sheriff to capture them shortly after the incident. Tex and Suzie had both been shot, but because of the excitement, neither one of them knew that they were injured. The bullet had pierced through Tex and caught Suzie in the shoulder. The wound was not deep, but the bullet was still in her. Tex had been shot in the chest and was losing a large amount of blood. His heart was racing and he was having difficulty with his breathing.

They took them to the North Houston Hospital, and Suzie had the bullet removed in the emergency room with just a few stitches. It could have been a lot worse, the doctor told her, if her husband had not stepped up to block the bullet. The doctor continued to explain that her husband had slowed the bullet down when he jumped in front of her, pushing her to the ground. Even though the bullet still penetrated her, it was just a flesh wound and she would heal up quickly. Her husband was not so lucky, and the doctor left Suzie crying in the waiting room, fearing the worst. Suzie, her dad, the cowboys, and members of the church prayed for Tex as he was in the emergency room getting the help he desperately needed. Now the hospital staff had to focus on Tex, who had suffered a severed vein and a collapsed lung as a result of the bullet wound.

As Tex laid on the gurney dying, a large group of people were moving around him; he saw his life flash before him. He quietly said to himself that he had lived an insignificant life and he would now die an insignificant death. *No one will miss me*, he thought, *and if it is my time to go, here I am.* He called upon the Lord and asked for help to get through his situation. He prayed for the Lord to be with Suzie and their baby if he should die. He ended his short but sincere prayer with, "Thy will be done and I place myself into your hands, my Lord my God." Tex had to undergo emergency surgery in an attempt to save his life. Three chest tubes were placed in the center of his chest cavity to drain the blood in hope of re-expanding the lungs.

CHAPTER 32

Who Am I?

In the distance of his subconscious, Tex could hear a familiar yet unfamiliar voice calling out to him. He wondered to himself if it was God calling him home. The voice was counting, *one, two, three, and wake up, Johnny B.* "Wake up!" shouted the man at the other end of the voice. The man behind the voice reached back and, with a hard blow, slapped Johnny's face, which brought him back into the world he had left behind so long ago.

Tammy's eyes welled with tears and showed her happiness to see him. She rushed over to him, hugged, and kissed him in order to express all of the love she had for him. She had missed her man terribly and was so excited to see him back from his trip inside his own mind. He had experienced a fugue in a most extraordinary way, but now he was snapping out of it and Tammy felt like things were going to get back to normal. He had come out of his hypnotic state which he had temporarily been placed in. Dr. S. was standing over him with a look of admiration and curiosity.

"Well, my boy, where have you been? We thought we had lost you for a minute. You see, we found you wandering down the I-10 interstate in a confused state of mind. You were lost and did not seem to know who you were or where you were going. We brought you back to the clinic and performed ECT on you to try and snap you out of your stupor. That did not work, and I went back over your notes from the clinic. I decided to try your therapy that has helped so many of our patients gain some type of normalcy. I decided to hypnotize you to give you a clean slate of memories. The idea you had written down in your notebook from the clinic seems to have some validity. You had been unconscious for a total of six months, and we had to start another IV to provide you with fluids and nutrition.

"Every day when the clinic was complete, Tammy and I worked on trying to hypnotize you to break through your unconscious state of mind. I think it finally took and we were able to bring you back out of your psychotic episode. We all know who you really are now due to the Switzerland Board of Psychology finally getting back to us on your lack of credentials. They stated that the real Dr. D. was still in Switzerland practicing medicine at the same facility he has been a part of for over twenty years. They exposed you for the imposter that you are. I must say, you put on quite a convincing act, and I was fooled completely, along with many others.

"Also, if you have any concerns about Tommy's wife, let me put them to rest. I am proud to announce that she is just fine and happier in her marriage than she has ever been. They are expecting their first child in a couple of months, and it is largely because of your therapy that you provided Tommy. Tammy is not too terribly upset with you and still wants to marry you if you still love her. The university is not pressing charges, and neither am I. After all, I owe you my life, and you did help tremendously with the clinic. Impersonating a physician and practicing medicine without a license is a serious offense, but we can conclude you were acting in desperation at the time. We just hope that you will abide by the following rules.

"Number one, continue to come to the clinic for help with your schizophrenia, therapy, and take your medication. Number two, please help our patients by sharing your experiences with them but no more hypnosis. Keep all conversations with the patients positive and let them know that there is help for them. Emphasize that they can live in this world that is just as strange to them as their appearance and idiosyncrasies are to us. Number three, we have set up a full scholarship for you to pursue any degree that you would like to try and achieve. You must come to school and get a degree of your choosing because the university feels like you have an incredible gift that should not be wasted due to inaccessibility of an education. Number four, marry Tammy because she loves you and it would be a good way to keep up with you and your progress. She will make you a good wife, and I know you love her just as much as she loves you. You guys belong together, and you seem to be inspirational to each other.

"I hope that these explanations ease your mind and answer all your questions. I think that with the stress of being responsible for a murder, impersonation of a doctor, marriage to one that you love under false pretenses, and attempting to explain everything to the police, that your mind just snapped. It could have happened to anybody with all of that guilt and pressure you succumbed to, locking your mind up in your head until we were able to break through. It was just too much pressure, but you look like you are doing a lot better now. Thank God.

"I would like to see you in my office next month. I have a lot of questions to ask you about the trip you took in your mind's eye while under the influence of hypnosis and ECT. I know Tammy has been waiting a long time for you to snap out of your state, and I will leave you two alone so that you two can get reacquainted. She will undoubtedly have questions, want to plan a wedding, honeymoon, and make other reasonable plans about the future of your home." After all the discussion, explanation, and other jargon put forth by the doctor to help Johnny B., better understanding his situation, he sat right up in his bed and said, "The name is Tex, Doc, and I just want to go home."

THE END

9 798822 956803